The Bourne Ultimatum

ROBERT LUDLUM

Level 6

Retold by David Maule
Series Editors: Andy Hopkins and Jocelyn Potter

Pearson Education Limited
Edinburgh Gate, Harlow,
Essex CM20 2JE, England
and Associated Companies throughout the world.

ISBN: 978-1-4082-6388-4

This edition first published by Pearson Education Ltd 2012
This edition arranged with the Orion Publishing Group Ltd, London

1 3 5 7 9 10 8 6 4 2

Illustrations by Chris King

Set in 11/14pt Bembo
Printed in China
SWTC/01

Published by Pearson Education Limited in association with
Penguin Books Ltd, and both companies being subsidiaries of Pearson PLC

Contents

Introduction

"Call his house. Tell David to take Marie and the children and get out of there!"

"What?"

"Somebody found us! Somebody looking for Jason Bourne."

"Do you know what you're saying, Alex?"

"You're damned right I do. It's Carlos. Carlos the Jackal!"

The Jackal is an international assassin, a professional terrorist, who kills for people who can pay his high fees. For years he and Jason Bourne have hunted each other, but now the Jackal is growing old. He wants to try one last time to kill his hated rival. Then Bourne will know—and the world will say—that he, Carlos, is the best. Bourne has two options: he can go into hiding with his family and live in fear, or he can find the Jackal and kill him. He chooses, as always, to take action.

Bourne's real name is David Webb and he works as a professor at a small university in Maine, in the United States. For years, since the events described in *The Bourne Supremacy*—also a Penguin Reader—he has led the quiet life of an academic. He has two children and is now past fifty, but he knows that for his own survival and the survival of his family he must become Jason Bourne again—and he must find the physical strength and skills of a much younger man.

Webb first became Jason Bourne in the 1970s, when he was working in Cambodia for the Central Intelligence Agency (CIA). In neighboring Vietnam, the war between the Americans and the North Vietnamese was coming to an end. One day, a plane from across the border killed Webb's first wife and their children. Crazy with anger, he ran away to Saigon, where he was asked to join a secret special operations group known as

Medusa. While working for Medusa, behind enemy lines, Webb met the original Jason Bourne. He met him and killed him, because Bourne was working for the North Vietnamese.

Years later, Webb uses the name Jason Bourne in a secret operation that goes badly wrong. He is shot in the head and loses his memory. However, his employers in the United States think he has gone out of their control and has stolen a lot of government money. They—and his real enemies—try to kill him. The story of how Bourne, with the help of a young Canadian woman named Marie, discovers who he is and defeats the assassins, is told in the first of the three best-known Bourne books: *The Bourne Identity*. This is also a Penguin Reader.

In *The Bourne Supremacy*, the second book in the series, Bourne is married to Marie, but is forced away from his quiet, normal life in Maine to Hong Kong. It is 1985, when Hong Kong is moving into its last period under British control. In 1997 it will become part of the People's Republic of China. Nobody is sure what the future might bring, and most of the action of the novel takes place in this dangerous situation of uncertainty.

The Bourne Ultimatum takes us from the United States to the islands of the Caribbean, then to Paris, and finally to the Soviet Union during its final years. This was a country ruled by the Communist Party and controlled by its security service, the KGB. In this tightly-run state, Bourne at last comes face to face with the Jackal. And against this background, the name "Medusa" is heard again. The young officers of Vietnam are now older men in senior positions. They still work closely together, but their aim now is money and power.

The Bourne Identity, The Bourne Supremacy, and *The Bourne Ultimatum* are all bestsellers and were made into movies starring Matt Damon. The stories in the movies, however, are very different from the books. In the movie of *The Bourne*

Ultimatum, Jason Bourne is hunted by the CIA; in the book, the CIA tries to help him. The movie, in fact, has very little in common with the book, except for the name of its main character and some details of his background.

Robert Ludlum was born in New York City in 1927 and grew up in New Jersey. His talents first led him in the direction of acting, and he appeared in a Broadway show at the age of sixteen. From 1945 to 1947 he served as a soldier in the South Pacific, and his first serious piece of writing was a 200-page description of his time there. However, after returning home and graduating from college, he continued with his acting career. In the 1950s he worked as a stage and television actor. He then became a producer of plays for theaters in New York and other cities.

His first novel, *The Scarlatti Inheritance*, appeared in 1971 and became a bestseller. This was followed by *The Osterman Weekend*, which was later made into a movie. The hero of the book, John Tanner, works with the CIA to discover a group of Soviet agents among his closest friends. This sets the style of Ludlum's heroes as strong, independent men who battle against organizations, sometimes secret ones. The action always takes place against a background of real-world events.

From the mid-1970s, Ludlum was a full-time writer. He wrote more than twenty novels. Over 200 million copies have been sold and the books have been translated into twenty-nine languages. Five of them have been filmed, and two more are in development.

Robert Ludlum died in Florida in 2001. Since then, however, a number of novels have appeared in his name, based on writing that was incomplete at the time of his death, and five more Bourne novels have been produced by the writer Eric Van Lustbader.

"That's fire, young man," answered Bourne softly.

Chapter 1 The Return of the Jackal

The summer night was hot in Baltimore. In the amusement park the music from the different attractions was loud, and people's faces and necks shone with sweat under the colored lights.

A thin middle-aged man, a walking stick gripped in his right hand, limped through the crowds. His name was Alexander Conklin and he had once been an officer in the Central Intelligence Agency. He was at this moment very anxious. He did not wish to be in this place at this time.

Suddenly, he stopped in shock, his eyes on a tall man about his own age. Morris Panov was walking toward him. *Why?* What had *happened?* Conklin looked around in every direction, knowing that he and Panov were being watched. It was too late to stop the psychiatrist from entering the center of the meeting ground but it might *not* be too late to get them both out! Conklin moved quickly forward, limping and swinging his walking stick against the crowd, hitting knees and pushing it at stomachs until people shouted and moved angrily away. He then rushed forward and shouted into Panov's face through the noise of the crowd.

"What the hell are *you* doing here?"

"The same as I think you are. David—or should I say *Jason*? That's what the message said."

"It's a trap!"

There was a scream that was louder than the angry crowd. Both Conklin and Panov immediately looked around. Only meters away, a woman had been shot in the throat. The crowd went crazy. Conklin turned, trying to see where the shot had come from, but saw only moving figures. He took hold of Panov and pulled him through the screaming, frightened bodies toward the far end of the park.

"My God!" shouted Panov. "Was that meant for one of *us*?"

"Maybe ... maybe not," replied Conklin breathlessly as the sound of police whistles was heard in the distance.

"You said it was a *trap*!"

"Because we both got a crazy message from David using a name he hasn't used in five years—*Jason Bourne*! And if I'm not mistaken, your message said that under *no* condition should we call his house."

"That's right."

"It's a trap. You move better than I do, so get out of here, run and find a telephone. Call his house. Tell David to take Marie and the children and get out of there!"

"*What?*"

"Somebody found us! Somebody looking for Jason Bourne."

"Do you know what you're saying, Alex?"

"You're damned right I do. It's Carlos. Carlos the Jackal! Now get out of here and don't go home! Take a room at the Brookshire Hotel in Baltimore under the name of—Morris, Phillip Morris. I'll meet you there later. Now *hurry*!"

♦

The car raced south, down a quiet road through the hills of New Hampshire. The driver was a tall man with a strong face and a look of anger in his eyes. Beside him sat his attractive wife, holding a baby of eight months. In the back seat was another child, a boy of five, asleep under a blanket. The father was David Webb, a university professor, but once part of Medusa, where he was known as Jason Bourne, the assassin.

"We knew it had to happen," said Marie St. Jacques Webb. "It was just a question of time."

"It's *crazy*!" Webb said quietly. "Everything's buried, top secret. How did anybody find Alex and Mo?"

"Alex doesn't know, but he'll start looking. There's no one

better than Alex—you said that yourself— "

"He's marked now—he's a dead man," said Webb.

"It's too soon to say that, David. 'He's the best there ever was'—those were your words."

"Yes, he may live, but not Mo. They'll take him and fill him up with drugs until he tells them about his whole life. Then they'll kill him and come after me ... after *us*, which is why you and the kids are going to the Caribbean."

"I'll send *them*, dear. Not me."

"*Stop* it! We agreed when Jamie was born. That's why we gave the money to your brother. We now own half of a hotel down a dirt road on an almost unknown island."

Marie looked at her husband and what she saw frightened her more than the thought of the Jackal. She was not looking at David Webb, the quiet university professor. She was staring at a man they both thought had disappeared from their lives forever.

♦

Alexander Conklin limped into the conference room at the Central Intelligence Agency in Langley, Virginia. He stood facing a long table, large enough to seat thirty people, but instead there were only three. One was Peter Holland, the gray-haired DCI: Director of Central Intelligence. On each side of him sat Casset and Valentino, his two deputy directors. All of them had worked with Conklin. They knew him well and trusted him, as he did them, but none appeared pleased to see him. The greetings were short and, instead of taking a seat near the DCI, Conklin pulled out a chair at the far end of the table and sat down.

"Now that we've said hello, can we get to the point, gentlemen?"

"That's not a very polite or friendly way to begin, Mr. Conklin," said the director.

"Just tell me why top secret information that puts a number of lives at risk was released."

"That couldn't happen, Alex, and you know it," said Casset.

"I don't know it and it did happen. A man who is owed more by this country than can ever be repaid is running in terror, with his wife and children. Some of the information in that file was passed on and it worries me deeply because my name is there … mine and Dr. Morris Panov's. We were the only two people known to be close to Jason Bourne. If anybody wants any part of that file it has to be approved by the top level here in Langley—that's you, gentlemen. And then I have to be contacted and approve it, or if I'm dead, Morris Panov. No one knows the rules better, because I wrote them, with the full authority of the President of the United States."

"That's a very high level, Mr. Conklin," said the director.

"Yes, and if I don't get some answers I'll take this straight to the White House and see what they think."

The two deputy directors started talking at once but Holland held up his hand for silence. He picked up the telephone on the table.

"Please ask Mr. DeSole to come to the conference room," he said.

"Yes, I remember DeSole," Conklin said. "He knows everything but if he can't pass it on, he says nothing—he doesn't lie. "

There was a knock on the door and a middle-aged man with glasses walked into the room. He crossed to Conklin's chair.

"Good to see you again. It's been two or three years now?"

"More like four, Steve," replied Conklin, shaking hands. "How's the keeper of the keys?"

"Oh, it's all done by computer now. I don't go on foreign trips with an armed guard any more."

"Sit down, Mr. DeSole," said the director. "At this end

of the table, so Alex can study us as we explain to him. This morning I received a phone call from Edward McAllister, chairman of the National Security Agency. McAllister was with you in Hong Kong, Mr. Conklin, wasn't he?"

"Yes, he was shot and wounded so badly that he almost died."

"He didn't tell me that, but he did say I should give our meeting with you top priority. He also told me about the file you are talking about, and its level of secrecy. I gave this information to Mr. DeSole, so I'll let him tell you what he has learned."

"It hasn't been touched, Alex," said DeSole quietly. "It's been unopened for four years, five months and twenty-one days."

"So what *happened*?" said Conklin softly.

"We have to look elsewhere," said the DCI. "But there's another thing. Most of the information about Bourne is still secret—even from us. I don't want to start opening files that were closed by the White House but there's little we can do to help if we're completely uninformed."

Conklin looked at each man, trying to come to a difficult decision. "Where do I begin?" he said.

"With this meeting?" suggested the director. "Why did you arrange it?"

Conklin looked down at the table for a moment, then lifted his head. "A woman was killed last night in an amusement park in Baltimore—"

"I read about it in the newspaper this morning," said DeSole.

"Were you involved?" asked the director.

"I was there—Morris Panov and I. We both received messages from Jason Bourne asking us to come to the amusement park at nine-thirty last night. When I saw Panov I knew something was wrong, so I got him out, but that poor woman was killed."

"What do you think of it all?" asked Valentino.

"I just don't know, Val. It was a trap, but what kind of trap? If the intention was to kill me, or Panov, how could a hired gunman miss at that distance? That's if my thinking is right."

"'Right,' Mr. Conklin," said the DCI, "meaning the assassin, Carlos the Jackal?"

"*Carlos?*" said DeSole. "What does he have to do with it?"

"Jason Bourne," answered Casset.

"Bourne was a violent criminal who was killed in the Far East five years ago, but Alex talks as if he was still alive."

"I think you should start at the beginning, Mr. Conklin," said the director. "Who *is* Jason Bourne?"

"As the world knew him, a man who never existed," replied Conklin. "Let's start by going back a number of years, to the war in Vietnam ..."

Chapter 2 Snake Lady

A gray Pontiac with a CIA driver picked Webb up at Washington National Airport and drove him into Virginia. The car turned into the drive of an expensive garden apartment complex. The guard obviously recognized the driver and waved him through as the heavy bar across the entrance was raised. Only then did the driver speak directly to Webb.

"This place is Agency property, sir. You couldn't be safer."

The driver pulled up outside a white two-floor villa. As Webb left the car and walked up the steps, the door opened.

"How do you like my temporary home?" said Conklin.

"Too neat and clean for you," Webb said.

They went inside and sat down.

"I've sent Marie and the kids off south—a long way south," Webb said. "I hired a Rockwell jet out of Logan Airport. They took off early this morning. And I've taken a suite at the

Mayflower Hotel."

"That's good," Conklin said. "But we have no information on how he found us."

"I've thought about it," Webb said. "It has to be Hong Kong. Some people knew and he's made one of them talk somehow."

Conklin thought for a moment. "It's possible," he said.

"Yes, but it doesn't matter. He's coming after me—that's the important thing. I have to go after *him*. He's trying to pull me out, so I have to pull him out first. And we'll do it according to your teaching."

"What do you mean?" asked Conklin.

"You once said that in order to set a trap you have to use a large part of the truth, even a dangerous amount."

"Yes, I think I said that once. What's the relevance here?"

"Medusa," said Webb quietly. "I want to use Medusa."

"Now you *are* out of your mind," responded Conklin. "That name is as secret as yours is—in fact, much more so."

"Snake Lady," Webb said quietly. "That's the key, isn't it?"

"You remembered?"

"Just this morning," replied Webb. "When Marie and the kids were in the air, suddenly my mind went back to Vietnam. Every officer in Command Headquarters who was connected to Medusa got himself a tattoo on the inside of his arm."

"Yes, a woman with snakes for hair. You refused to have one, but the others were like kids with a secret code."

"They weren't kids, Alex. More than a few millionaires were made in Command Saigon. The real kids were being wounded and killed in the jungles while a lot of officers in the south opened Swiss bank accounts."

"Careful, David. You could be speaking of some very important people in our government."

"Who are they?" asked Webb quietly.

"I've got some ideas, but no proof. Just possibilities, based on the way they live, on property they shouldn't be able to afford, or positions that are a long way above their talents."

"You're describing a network," said Webb, his voice hard. "Make a list, Alex."

"What the *hell* has any of this to do with Carlos?"

"Let's say you find three or four names. We apply pressure. We give them a message: A former Medusan has had a mental breakdown and he's going to tell everything. He's got the information—names, crimes, the numbers of secret Swiss bank accounts, everything. Then word is passed on that there's somebody who wants this dangerous man more than they do."

"Carlos the Jackal," said Conklin softly. "And then word gets out calling for a meeting between Carlos's people and the Medusans to discuss assassinating the man. The Medusans can't come after you themselves because of their high official positions but they can find out your identity."

"And Carlos won't suspect them because whoever meets with his messengers has to be a real person in a high position."

"I hear a man from the past, a man who never was."

"Oh, he *was*, Alex. And now Jason Bourne is back."

♦

The senator swore out loud as he turned off the shower and walked to the phone on the wall.

"This is Armbruster," he said. "What is it?"

"Snake Lady, Senator."

"Oh, my *God*!" Armbruster's voice was a sudden cry of panic. On the other end of the line, Conklin smiled. Then the senator controlled himself. "I have no idea what you're talking about. What's a Snake whatever-it-is—I've never heard of it."

"Well, hear it now, Mr. Medusa. Somebody's got it all, everything. Dates, stolen war supplies, Swiss banks."

"You're not making sense! You're talking garbage!"

"And you're on the list, Senator. That man must have spent fifteen years putting it together and now he wants payment for all that work, or he tells everything."

"Who? Who *is* he, for God's sake?"

"We're working on it. Stay tight. We'll be back in touch."

As Armbruster hung up the phone, he stared at the small, ugly tattoo on the underside of his arm.

Over in Virginia, Alex Conklin studied his list and made a mark after the name of Albert Armbruster. After another call he added a mark to that of General Norman Swayne, chief of military purchasing at the Pentagon. He called a senior advisor to the President, who had no idea what he was talking about, so Conklin crossed out his name. He then called Phillip Atkinson, ambassador to Great Britain, on a very secure line. Conklin was a skilled professional. He let his words lead to other words, encouraging Atkinson to talk. At the end of the conversation he also had the names of James Teagarten, commander of NATO, and Jonathan "Jack" Burton, chairman of the Joint Chiefs of Staff*.

Snake Lady. Medusa. A network.

♦

In a hotel suite on the third floor of Boston's Ritz-Carlton Hotel, a very tall man in a well-cut suit came rushing out of the bedroom and answered the door.

"Come in. Quickly! Did you bring the information?"

"Oh, yes, yes," answered the visitor, a thin, older man in a very old suit. "How grand you look, Randolph," he continued. "And how grand this place is—so suitable for such a famous professor."

"The information, please," insisted Dr. Randolph Gates,

* Joint Chiefs of Staff: a group of military leaders who advise the government of the United States

Harvard professor, expert in company law, and highly paid consultant to numerous industries.

"Oh, give me a moment, my old friend. It's been a long time since I've been *near* a hotel suite. I certainly haven't stayed in one. How things have changed for us over the years. I read about you frequently and I've watched you on television."

"You could have been in the same position, you know," interrupted the impatient Gates. "You were a respected judge. Unfortunately, you didn't play by the rules."

"There are lots of rules. I just chose the wrong ones."

"I haven't time to talk about that. The information, please."

"Oh, yes ... of course. Well, first the money was delivered to me. I reached the engineer at the telephone company, who was very happy at your—excuse me—*my* generosity. I then took the information he gave me to that private detective."

"Please," interrupted the famous professor of law. "What did the man find out?"

"Well, he worked at a very high hourly rate. I mean, I had to use some of my own fee to pay him, so I think we should discuss an adjustment, don't you?"

"Who the hell do you think you are? I sent you 3,000 dollars! 500 for the telephone man and 1500 for the private detective—"

"He does good work. Do we discuss my fee or do I leave?"

They discussed the fee. At the end of an angry conversation, the former judge had the promise of a check for fifteen thousand dollars and Gates had the information that a woman with a five-year-old child and a baby had flown out of Boston's Logan Airport. The jet they used was on government business under maximum security. Its destination was Blackburne Airport on the Caribbean island of Montserrat. He also learned that Marie St. Jacques's brother Johnny owned a hotel on the island of Tranquility, not far from Montserrat.

After his visitor left, Gates made a call to Paris.

An hour later, Brendan Prefontaine, former high court judge, walked out of the Boston Five Bank with 15,000 dollars in his pocket. It was an exciting experience for a man who had lived with very little money for the past thirty years. Since his release from prison he had rarely had more than fifty dollars on his person. This was a very special day.

But it was more than very special. It was also very disturbing, because he had never thought for a minute that Randolph Gates would pay him anything near the amount he demanded. Gates had made an enormous error in doing so, because he had crossed the line from nasty and greedy to possibly dangerous. Prefontaine had no idea who the woman and the children were, or what their relationship was to Randolph Gates, but he knew that Gates intended to harm them.

It might, therefore, be profitable for Prefontaine to find out a little more. 15,000 today might become 50,000 tomorrow, if he flew to the island of Montserrat and began asking questions.

Besides, thought the judge, he had not had a vacation in years.

♦

The Air France steward rolled the wheelchair slowly toward the 747 jet in Paris's Orly Airport. The thin woman in the chair was elderly and an equally elderly man walked beside her.

"He is here, Captain," announced the steward at the aircraft's entrance. The captain reached for the woman's hand and touched it to his lips, then stood straight and shook hands with the old man.

"It is an honor, sir," said the captain in his native language. "If there's anything the crew and I can do to make the flight more comfortable for you, please don't hesitate to ask."

"You are very kind."

"We are all in your debt, all of France."

"It was nothing, really—"

Later, as he sat in his seat drinking wine, the old "hero of France"—whose only heroics in World War II were based on theft and survival—reached into his pocket for his papers. The passport had his picture on it, but that was the only thing he recognized. The rest—name, date and place of birth, occupation—were all unfamiliar, and the attached list of honors was impressive. He had been assured that the individual originally possessing the name had no living relatives, few friends, and had disappeared from his apartment in Marseilles, supposedly on a world trip from which he was unlikely to return.

The old man looked at the name—he must remember it and respond whenever it was spoken. It should not be difficult, because it was such a common name. And so he repeated it silently to himself again and again.

Jean Pierre Fontaine, Jean Pierre Fontaine, Jean Pierre …

Chapter 3 The Tranquility Hotel

"I talked to Marie," said Conklin from the Agency house in Virginia.

"How is she—and the children?" asked Bourne at a gas station pay phone on the outskirts of Manassas, in the same state.

"They're all fine. They're at the hotel. She wanted to hear about you. I said you were safe and told her not to worry."

"Thanks for that. They should be safe at the hotel. It's on the beach. The only way to get there except by water is up a dirt road. Everything is flown in by plane or brought over by boat."

"And the beach is guarded, she said. Johnny isn't taking any chances."

"It's why I sent them down there. I'll call her later."

"Did you go to see Armbruster?" Conklin asked.

"Yes. You told him to expect Cobra, and I said I was Cobra, and he never questioned it. Of course, I know enough about the old days in Saigon, and some of the other people in Medusa, so he believed I was on the inside."

"So, did you learn anything?"

"Well, he's rich. He talked about having a hundred million dollars in Zurich. He regularly gets a list of the companies they're taking control of. He said that in six months 'we' would have all the controls we needed in Europe. Alex, what are we dealing with?"

There was silence on the line and Jason Bourne did not interrupt. David Webb wanted to shout out in anger and confusion, but there was no point. Webb did not matter. Finally, Conklin spoke.

"I think we're dealing with something we can't handle," he said softly. "This information has to go to Peter Holland, David. We can't keep it to ourselves."

"God damn you, you're not talking to David!" Bourne did not raise his voice in anger. He did not have to. His tone was enough. "This isn't going anywhere unless or until I say it does and I may not ever say it. Understand me, Alex, I don't owe anybody anything, especially not the important people in the city. They gave my wife and me too much trouble! Don't stand in my way. Don't, for God's sake!"

"I hear you," said Conklin. "I don't know whether I'm hearing David or Jason Bourne, but I hear you. But we have to move fast and I'm talking to Bourne now. What's next? Where are you?"

"About ten kilometers from General Swayne's house," replied Bourne, breathing deeply. "I'll get there while it's light so I can see what it's like from the road—then after dark I'll pay him a surprise visit."

"Be careful. He may have alarms and dogs, things like that."

"I'm prepared," said Jason Bourne. "I did some shopping."

♦

The Tranquility Hotel had been cut out of three rocky hills above a long beach. Two rows of villas with balconies extended from each side of a large circular building of heavy stone and thick glass. The villas were connected by a path bordered by bushes and low lamps. Waiters wheeled room-service tables along the path, delivering food and drinks to Tranquility's guests, most of whom now sat on their balconies enjoying the end of the Caribbean day. And as darkness fell, other people quietly appeared on the beach. These were the armed guards, each dressed in a dark brown tropical uniform and with a MAC-10 machine pistol on his waist. On the opposite side of each jacket and hooked to the cloth was a pair of Zeiss Ikon 8x10 binoculars, continually used to look out into the darkness.

On the large circular balcony of the villa nearest the main building, an elderly woman sat in a wheelchair drinking a glass of white wine. She heard the voice of her husband talking with the nurse inside, then the sound of his quiet footsteps as he walked out to join her.

"I can't believe we are living in this place," she said.

"Neither can I."

The telephone inside the villa rang. He turned. "The nurse will get it," he said.

"She's strange," added the old woman. "I don't trust her."

"She works for our employer."

"Really?"

"Yes. She will pass on his instructions."

The uniformed nurse appeared in the doorway. "Sir, that was Paris." She turned and signaled for him to follow, then crossed the room and unlocked the drawer of a table. He walked over to her and glanced down at what was in the drawer. Side by side were a pair of surgical gloves, a handgun with a silencer attached to the barrel, and a straight razor.

"These are your tools," said the woman, handing him the key, "and your targets are in the last villa on this row. You must make yourself familiar with the area by taking long walks on the path, as old men do for their health, and you must kill them. You will do this wearing the gloves and firing the gun into each head. Then each throat must be cut—"

"Mother of God, the children's?"

"Those are the orders."

"The orders are disgusting!"

"Do you wish me to pass that on to our employer?"

Fontaine looked over at the balcony door, at his wife in the wheelchair. "No, no, of course not … When must this be done?"

"Within the next thirty-six hours."

"Then what?"

"You may stay here until your wife dies."

♦

Brendan Patrick Prefontaine was again astonished. Though he had no reservation, the front desk of the Tranquility Hotel treated him like a very important visitor, then, only moments after he had booked himself into a villa, told him that he already *had* a villa and asked how the flight from Paris was. Eventually, the misunderstanding became clear, and the former judge from Boston was taken to a lovely small house overlooking the Caribbean.

When he was settled, his casual clothes in the closet, the craziness continued. A bottle of wine, some fresh-cut flowers, and a box of Belgian chocolates arrived. A little later, a confused room-service waiter returned to remove the chocolates, apologizing for the fact that they were for another villa. The waiter was followed by the assistant manager, a Mr. Pritchard, who explained that the problem was caused by the similarity between his name, Prefontaine, and that of an important guest from Paris, a Mr. Fontaine. The judge accepted his apology, although he would rather have had the chocolates.

Chapter 4 The Farm

Darkness had fallen on Manassas as Bourne crept through the woods around General Norman Swayne's farm. He reached a fence—high, with thick crossed wire. Bourne wondered why a general who worked in an office would build something so expensive around a farm. It was not designed to keep animals in, but to keep people out.

Bourne knew there would be no electric alarms because the animals and birds would set them off repeatedly. He pulled his small wire cutters out of his back pocket and started to work on the wire. With each cut he again understood, confirmed by his heavy breathing and the sweat on his face, that he was now past fifty and his body knew it. It was something not to think about because there were Marie and the children, and there was nothing he couldn't do if he wanted to. David Webb had gone from his mind; only the hunter Jason Bourne remained.

He was through! He gripped the fence and pulled the opening toward him, then crawled inside. He stood up, listening, his eyes moving in every direction. He saw, through the branches of the trees, the lights of the large house. Slowly he made his way toward what he knew was the circular drive. Then, reaching the edge of the road, he lay flat under a tree, collecting his thoughts and his breath as he studied the scene in front of him. Suddenly, there was a flash of light on his far right. A door had been opened. It belonged to a smaller, separate house—a log cabin.

Two men and a woman came out and were talking ... no, they were not just talking, they were arguing—heatedly. Bourne took the binoculars out of his pocket and put them up to his eyes. He studied the three people, knowing that the medium-sized, protesting man was the Pentagon's General Swayne, and the woman with dark hair was his wife. But what fascinated him was the tall, overweight man nearest the door. He *knew* him! He could not remember from where or when, which was certainly not unusual, because his memory often failed him. But he knew that he hated him, and that was *not* usual. He could not explain it because no connection came to him. Where were the images, the brief flashes from the past, that often filled his mind? They did not come; he only knew that the man he saw through his binoculars was his enemy.

Then that huge man did a strange thing. He put his large left arm around the shoulders of Swayne's wife, his right arm waving in the air as he shouted at the general. Swayne turned around and walked across to his house. The large man released the general's wife and spoke to her. She nodded, touched her lips against his, and ran after her husband. The other man walked back into the cabin and closed the door, removing the light.

Bourne knew that he had to reach the man who had been part of his forgotten past. He slowly got to his feet and, moving from one tree to another, made his way toward the cabin. He stopped, dropping to the ground, when he heard the sound of wheels. Within seconds he saw a small, strangely shaped vehicle like a three-wheeled golf cart racing out of the shadows of the circular drive. It seemed designed for both high speed and balance, and thick glass surrounded the driver on all sides—glass that Bourne knew would stop a bullet. Then a second three-wheeled cart came out of the shadows behind the cabin.

It stopped only meters from the first one and these words came from an unseen speaker: "Secure the gates. Release the dogs and continue your rounds."

The carts swung away in opposite directions and Bourne reached into his back pocket and pulled out his dart gun. If the dogs hunted together, he would have no choice—he would have to climb the fence. The gun could stop two animals, not more; there would be no time to reload.

Suddenly, a large black dog raced past on the drive. It didn't slow down as it passed him; it didn't pick up the human smell. It was on its way somewhere. Then another dog appeared, this one long-haired. It did slow down, but as if it was trained to halt at a specific area. Standing motionless, Bourne understood. These were trained male attack dogs, each with its own territory. It was a practice used by landowners in the Far East. Vietnam ... Medusa. It was coming back to him! Half-remembered images—a young, powerful man in uniform. That *same man*, older, larger, had been in the viewfinder of his binoculars only moments ago! And years ago that same man had promised supplies and brought nothing. Bourne remembered taking his gun out and pushing the barrel against the man's forehead.

"One more word and you're dead, Sergeant." The man had *been* a sergeant. "You bring us supplies by five o'clock tomorrow morning or I'll get to Saigon and personally blow your head off." They got the supplies.

Bourne's thoughts came back to the present. The long-haired attack dog was suddenly circling in the road, its nose picking up the human smell. Within seconds it found the right direction and ran through the bushes, its teeth white in the darkness. Bourne moved back to the fence, raising the dart gun with his right hand, his left arm bent and extended. The angry animal jumped. Bourne fired first one dart and then the other. As the darts struck the dog, Bourne wrapped his arm around its head, pulling the head to one side while swinging his right knee up into the animal's body to push away the sharp-nailed feet. It was finished in moments—moments of quietening anger until the dog fell asleep in Bourne's arms. He lowered it to the ground and once again waited, afraid to move until he knew that none of the other animals had heard.

There was no sound from them, but Bourne heard one of the carts approaching. It stopped near the front gate. The driver opened the door and began to throw pieces of food to the black dog. Bourne knew that he had to stop the cart and force the driver outside without giving him any reason to use his radio to call for help. He looked at the sleeping dog at his feet. Place it in the road? No, the driver might assume it had been shot from the other side of the fence and call the house. What could he *do*?

He looked around and saw a fallen branch on the ground. He crossed quickly to it and pulled it toward the drive. To lay it across the drive might appear too obvious a trap, but partially on the road might work. The grounds were neat and the guards under the big man's command would want to avoid criticism. Bourne swung the branch around and pushed it around two meters into the road. He heard the door of the cart shut; the vehicle rolled forward, gathering speed as Bourne raced back into the darkness of the tree.

The driver's single headlight lit up the branch on the road. He slowed down and approached it cautiously, as if he were unsure what it was. Then he stopped, opened his door, stepped out on the drive, and walked around the front of the cart.

"Big Rex, you're one bad dog," said the driver, in a quiet, very Southern voice. "What did you pull out of there, you stupid animal? … Rex? *Rex*, you come here!"

"Stay completely still and put your arms out in front of

you," said Jason Bourne, walking into view.

"My God! Who are you?"

"Somebody who doesn't give a damn whether you live or die," said Bourne.

Half an hour later, with all six attack dogs drugged and carried to their sleeping place, Bourne opened the entrance gate and let the two guards leave. By now they believed that he was working for a higher authority, and he had also given them each three hundred dollars. They knew he was not a terrorist because they were still alive, and they were happy enough to walk off down the road.

Bourne used one of the carts to drive most of the way to the cabin, then crept forward and looked through the window. The huge sergeant was sitting in an armchair watching television.

Bourne walked around the cabin to the front door. He knocked with his left hand; in his right was an automatic.

"It's open, Rachel!" shouted the voice from within.

Bourne twisted the handle and pushed the door back. He walked inside.

"No!" roared the sergeant, pushing his great body out of the chair. "You! You're a ghost! You're dead!"

"Try again," said Jason Bourne of Medusa. "The name's Flanagan, isn't it? That's what comes to mind."

"You're dead!" repeated the general's assistant, screaming, his eyes wide in panic. "You were killed in Hong Kong … four, five years ago!"

"You checked?"

"We know—I know!"

"You've got connections in the right places, then."

"You're Bourne—I don't believe this. You're the one Swayne called 'Cobra'!"

"I know, it's confusing."

"You're one of us! How did you get in here? Where are the

guards, the dogs? Where are they?"

"The dogs are asleep, drugged, and I sent the guards home."

Suddenly, in the distance, there was a gunshot. Bourne spun around … then kept turning. All the way around! The huge sergeant was jumping at him, his big hands sliding over Bourne's shoulders. Bourne kicked with his right foot, catching the sergeant's side while he crashed the barrel of the automatic into the base of the man's neck. Flanagan fell forward onto the floor and Bourne hammered his foot into the man's head, stunning him into silence—a silence that was broken by the continuous screams of a woman racing outside toward the door of the cabin. Within seconds, General Norman Swayne's wife burst into the room, stepping back at the sight in front of her, gripping the back of the nearest chair, unable to contain her panic.

"He's dead!" she screamed, falling to the floor and reaching for her lover. "He shot himself, Eddie! He killed himself!"

Jason Bourne walked to the door of the strange cabin that held so many secrets. Watching his two prisoners, he closed it. The woman cried but they were not tears of sorrow, only fear. The sergeant shook his head, raising it, his expression a mixture of anger and puzzlement.

An hour later, Alex Conklin sat back in his chair, the phone in his hand, shocked by Jason Bourne's astonishing information.

"So where are Flanagan and Swayne's wife now?" he said.

"Gone. I let them go—they'd told me everything they knew. Now you've got to make sure that no one finds out!"

"All right, all right. There's a doctor in Falls Church that we've used before in special operations. I'll contact him. I'll also get somebody to take away the dogs. Open the gates."

"OK," said Bourne. "Now put me on tape. I'll tell you everything Flanagan told me. Hurry. I've got a lot to do."

"You're on tape."

Reading from the list he had written down, Bourne spoke quickly. There were the names of seven frequent guests at the general's dinner parties; then came the license plates from much more serious twice-monthly meetings. Last was the unlisted telephone number in New York that Flanagan had to call in an emergency. There was no name—only a machine that took messages. "That has to be priority one, Alex."

"We'll find out whose number it is," said Conklin. "The licenses are no problem and I'll have Casset run the names through the computers without telling DeSole."

"And Swayne? We've got to keep the death quiet until we find out who they all are and we can start a wave of fear rolling. Then we suggest the Carlos solution."

"I don't know—I can fool the doctor for a day or two but after that he'll want somebody higher than me to approve it. Maybe we should tell Peter Holland and ask him to approve the delay."

"No," said Bourne. "Give me two days—*get* me two days!"

Within an hour, Dr. Ivan Jax arrived at the Swayne's house. He turned off the engine, grabbed his medical bag, and got out of the car.

"I'm your doctor," he said, walking up the steps. "Our friend didn't give your name, but I guess I'm not supposed to have it."

"I guess not," agreed Bourne, extending a hand in a surgical glove as Jax approached.

They entered the house and Bourne watched while the doctor quickly, expertly, worked on the body, mercifully wrapping the head in bandages. Without explaining, he cut away parts of the general's clothing, examining those parts of the body beneath the fabric. Finally, he carefully rolled the body off the chair and onto the floor.

"Are you finished in here?" he asked, looking at Bourne.

"I've searched the room, Doctor, if that's what you mean."

"Yes … I want this room locked up. No one must enter it

after we leave until our friend says they can."

"I certainly can't guarantee that," said Bourne.

"Then *he'll* have to."

"Why?"

"Your general didn't kill himself. He was murdered."

Bourne called Conklin.

"The woman," said Alex Conklin. "From everything you told me, it had to be Swayne's wife. My God!"

"It doesn't change anything, but it looks that way," agreed Bourne. "But if she did kill her husband, she didn't tell Flanagan, and that doesn't make sense."

"No, it doesn't ..." Conklin paused, then spoke quickly. "Let me talk to Ivan—the doctor."

"He's gone. He put the body into his car and left a few minutes ago. He said he'd call you later and explain. He wants to get out of here and no one's to come into this room after I leave—until you inform the police."

"I've got to find a way of keeping everybody away from there. It's almost impossible."

"It's perfect. Our little game will start here."

Bourne hung up the telephone, then turned and glanced around the general's study. Since Flanagan and Rachel Swayne had left almost three hours ago, he had searched every part of it, as well as the dead guard's separate bedroom on the second floor. He had placed the items he intended to take on the coffee table; he studied them now.

There were three small notebooks, all the same size. The first was an appointments book; the second a personal telephone book; the last was a diary. With these were a few notes that Swayne had written, and his wallet. It seemed Bourne had found nothing very useful, nothing that connected with the modern Medusa. So he started searching the room again, this time taking more time.

Fourteen minutes later he came to the window and found it was covered with spots of blood. Not only that, but it was open—just a little, but open. Bourne looked closely and saw what kept it from closing. The end of the left curtain had been pulled out and was now stuck beneath the lower frame. Bourne stepped back, puzzled but not really surprised. This was what he had been looking for—the missing piece in the complex puzzle that was the death of Norman Swayne.

Somebody had climbed out that window after the shot that had blown the general's head apart. Somebody who knew the house and the grounds … and the dogs. A killer from Medusa.

Who? Who had been here? Flanagan … Swayne's wife? They would know, they had to know. Bourne picked up the telephone on the desk.

"Yes," answered Conklin.

"It wasn't Swayne's wife. It was somebody from Medusa who left by the window. But Flanagan and Swayne's wife must have known who was here. Pick them up and hold them—they lied to me."

"Sorry—I can't do that. They've disappeared."

"That's crazy. If I know you, you've had them followed since they left here."

"Electronically, not physically. They booked seats on the ten P.M. flight to London."

"London?" interrupted Bourne. "They told me they were going the other way, to the Pacific. To Hawaii."

"That's probably where they are going because they didn't check in for the London flight. We need to bring in Peter Holland."

"No, not yet! Give me the two days, Alex, please."

"I'll do the best I can."

Chapter 5 The Storm

The old man now known as Jean Pierre Fontaine cried silently as he knelt beside the bed, his face close to his wife's, his tears falling on the cold flesh of her arm. She was dead, and the note by her white hand said it all: *Now we are both free, my love.*

They were both free. She from the terrible pain, he from the price demanded by the Jackal for the comfort of her last days. He had known for months that his wife had pills which would end her life quickly if the pain became too great. He had frequently searched for them but he had never found them. There was a small box beside the bed, and it was empty.

Footsteps. The nurse! She had come out of her room, but she must not see his wife lying dead! Fontaine pushed himself up from the bed, wiped his eyes, and hurried to the door. The nurse stood just outside, her arm raised to knock.

"*Sir!* ... You surprised me."

Jean Pierre stepped out, quickly closing the door behind him.

"Regine is finally asleep," he whispered. "This terrible storm has kept her up for most of the night."

"To business," said the nurse, walking away from the door. "Are you prepared?"

"It will be a matter of minutes," replied Fontaine, heading for the table where his killing equipment lay in the locked drawer.

"There is a slight change in the course of action."

"Oh?" the old Frenchman said. "At my age changes are not welcome."

"These are orders from Paris. Do you wish to question them?"

"No." Fontaine shook his head.

"So, listen—there will be a fire in Villa Fourteen, three away from ours. There will no doubt be a great deal of confusion, with the storm and everybody shouting and calling for help. That will be your signal. Use the confusion, get through, and kill the woman and her children. But don't go immediately. It will take me some time—five minutes, maybe twenty—to do what I have to do. Wait until I return to Villa Eleven before you leave."

"May I ask—it will take you five minutes, maybe twenty, to do what?"

"You're a fool, old man. What must be done."

"Of course."

The nurse pulled her raincoat around her and walked to the front door of the villa.

"Get your equipment together and be out of here in three minutes," she commanded.

The door swung back with the wind as the woman opened it. She went outside into the heavy rain, pulling it shut behind her. Astonished and confused, the old Frenchman stood still, trying to make sense of what was happening. The nurse was also a killer. So why had he been sent thousands of kilometers to do the work that another person could do just as well, and without the pretence of his arrival?

Fontaine walked rapidly to the nurse's bedroom door and opened it. He began to pull apart the woman's room—suitcase, closet, clothes, bed, dressing table, writing desk … the desk. The drawer was locked. A heavy lamp sat on the desk, a thick metal base. He picked it up, pulling out the cord, and hit the drawer hard. He pulled it open and stared in horror at what he saw.

Next to each other in a plastic case were two hypodermic needles. They were filled with yellowish liquid—he did not need to know the chemicals. Liquid death in the veins.

Nor did he have to be told for whom they were intended. He pictured the two bodies beside each other in bed—it would have looked as if he and his wife had decided to die together. How thoroughly the Jackal had planned everything. But this wasn't the contract that the old man had with his employer. His wife was supposed to die naturally, when her time came.

As the old Frenchman went outside, the heavy rain fell, the blasts of wind throwing him off balance as he made his way up the path toward Villa Fourteen. He wiped his face with his left hand, his right hand gripping the weapon, a gun lengthened by a silencer.

Stop her! What was she *doing*? What did the fire she talked about *mean*? ... Then he saw it—a huge burst of flame in a window of Villa Fourteen!

Fontaine reached the front door, but it was locked. He raised the handgun, fired twice, and blew the lock apart.

Inside. The screams came from beyond the door of the main bedroom. The old Frenchman moved toward it, his legs unsteady. With what strength he had left, he kicked the door open and saw a scene that he knew had to come from hell.

The nurse, with Prefontaine's head in a wire, was forcing her victim down into the gasoline fire on the floor.

"*Stop!*" screamed the man known as Jean Pierre Fontaine. "*Enough! Now! You are dead!*"

Through the rising, spreading flames, the Frenchman fired and the nurse died.

♦

The storm had blown away when the early morning light broke over the eastern horizon. The first boats slowly moved out toward the fishing grounds, because the catch of the day meant one more day's survival. Marie, her brother, and the two old men were around a table on the balcony of an unoccupied villa. Over coffee, they had been talking for most of an hour. The old, false hero of France, who had finally betrayed his betrayer and told them everything he knew, had been assured that all the correct arrangements would be made for his wife. If it was possible, he wanted her to be buried on the islands.

"It's possible," said Johnny St. Jacques. "Because of you, my sister's alive."

"Because of me, young man, she might have died."

"Would you have killed me?" asked Marie.

"If I had not seen the needles? I don't know. I might have felt that I owed the Jackal your death, but certainly not the children's."

"God, you *are* a killer," said the brother quietly.

"I am many things. I don't ask forgiveness in this world."

"Many of us need forgiveness," remarked Brendan Patrick Prefontaine, former judge in Boston, as he touched the raw, tender skin of his neck below his burned white hair. "You see in front of you a criminal, justly tried and justly convicted."

Marie looked at him. "I don't understand why you came here," she said.

"Well, as I told you, the man who paid me to find out where you'd gone also paid me a large sum of money to keep the information to myself. So I thought, if the little I knew brought so much, much more might come if I learned a little more."

"I want the name of your client," said Marie.

"We don't need that," said St. Jacques. "Conklin knows it. And we don't need the judge here."

"Maybe we do," said Marie. "He could support Conklin's story when we tell it to certain people in Washington."

"I would be happy to," said Prefontaine. "I'm with you."

The telephone rang inside the villa. Johnny St. Jacques rose out of his chair but was blocked by his sister, who raced through the doors into the living room. She picked up the phone.

"*David?*"

"It's Alex," said the breathless voice on the line. "God, I've had this thing on redial for three hours! Are you all right?"

"There was a storm. It knocked out the phones. What about *David?* We need him—the Jackal will be here *tomorrow!*"

"What? How do you know."

"An old man told me … never mind. Just tell David to get here."

"David will be there, you know that."

"Yes, I do … because he's Jason Bourne."

Chapter 6 Night Fight

It was ten o'clock in the morning and they held each other tightly, but there was no time for talk—only the brief comfort of being together, safe together, secure in the knowledge that they knew things that the Jackal did not know and that knowledge gave them an enormous advantage. But it was only an advantage, not a guarantee, and Marie and the children were being flown south to Guadeloupe's Basse-Terre island. They would stay there with the Webbs' housekeeper, Mrs. Cooper, all under guard until they were called back to Tranquility. Marie objected, but Bourne would not give in.

Now they stood on the dock, two sea planes in the water at the far end. One had brought Bourne directly to Tranquility from Antigua. The other was ready for the flight to Guadeloupe, with Mrs. Cooper and the children already inside.

"Hurry, Marie," added Bourne. "I want to ask these two old men some questions."

A few hours later, in a dark storage room on the third floor of the Tranquility Hotel, Bourne and the old Frenchman sat in front of a window overlooking the east and west paths of the hotel grounds. Each man held a pair of binoculars, watching the people walking on the paths and down the stone stairs leading to the beach.

Suddenly, the door opened and Judge Brendan Prefontaine walked quickly, breathlessly inside.

"He's here," he said. "Three of St. Jacques's men, down the

beach to the east, couldn't be reached by radio. St. Jacques sent a guard to find them and the man just returned. All three were killed, each with a bullet in his throat."

"The Jackal!" said the Frenchman. "It's his signature. He is announcing his arrival."

♦

The steel band played as the remaining guests finished their dinners and moved through to the dance floor. St. Jacques had provided some loud entertainment for those guests who had stayed in the hotel. Very few had left after the fire and the deaths. Most thought the killings were just an isolated incident, and were determined to continue their vacations. Some were old friends of St. Jacques and loyalty kept them in place.

In St. Jacques's office, Bourne and Fontaine stood up as a strong-looking black woman in a nurse's uniform entered the room.

"Very good, my child, you look wonderful," said the Frenchman. "Remember now, I'll be holding your arm as we walk and talk, but when I squeeze you and raise my voice, telling you to leave me alone, you'll do as I say. Correct?"

"Yes, sir. I must hurry away, quite angry with you for being so impolite."

"That's it. There's nothing to be afraid of. It's just a game. We want to talk to somebody who is very shy."

"Are we ready?" asked Bourne.

"We're ready," replied the Frenchman, smiling pleasantly at the very puzzled young woman. "What are you going to do with all the money you're earning tonight, my dear?"

The girl smiled shyly. "I have a good boyfriend. I'm going to buy him a fine present."

The plan was simple to prepare and, like most good plans, however complex, simple to carry out. Old Fontaine's walk through the grounds of the Tranquility Hotel had been exactly mapped out. It began with Fontaine and the young woman returning to his villa, presumably to check his sick wife before his normal evening walk. They stayed on the lighted main path.

Two of St. Jacques's guards moved through hidden routes in the bushes, always near them. Bourne followed the second man, his radio on *Receive*, listening to the angry words of Fontaine.

"Where is that other nurse—that lovely girl who takes care of my woman? Where is she? I haven't seen her all day."

Bourne raised his head above a low wall and suddenly there were lights, *colored* lights. They had reached the path to an old church, and the red and blue lights lit the way to a place that the hotel's guests sometimes liked to visit. It was the last destination before the return route back to Fontaine's villa. St. Jacques had put a third guard there to prevent entrance. Then Bourne heard the words over the radio—*the* words that would send the false nurse racing away.

"Get away from me!" shouted Fontaine. "I don't like you."

Up ahead, the two guards were hiding side by side. They turned and looked at Bourne. He knew that from that moment, all decisions were his.

The unexpected rarely disturbed Bourne; it did now. Had Fontaine made a mistake? Had the old man forgotten about the guard on the path and mistaken him for the Jackal's contact?

Then another possibility came to Bourne's mind. Had the guard been killed or bribed, replaced by another? Bourne rose to his feet. What he saw stunned him!

Fontaine didn't move, his mouth open in shock, his wide eyes disbelieving, as another old man in a brown suit approached him and threw his arms around the old "hero of France." Fontaine pushed the man away in panic and puzzlement. The words burst out of the radio in Bourne's pocket.

"Claude! What a surprise! You are here!"

The old friend replied in a shaking voice. "It is a privilege our employer permitted me. To see my sister for a final time, and to give comfort to my friend, her husband."

"He brought you here? But of course, he did!"

"I must take you to him. The great man wishes to speak to you."

"But she's *dead*! She took her own life last night. *He* intended to kill us both."

Shut off your radio! screamed Bourne in the silence of his thoughts. It was too late. The door of the church opened and a man walked out into the colored lights. He was young, muscular, and blond. Was the Jackal training somebody to take his place?

"Come with me, please," said the blond man, his French gentle but commanding. "You," he added, addressing the old man in the brown suit, "stay where you are. At the slightest sound, fire your gun … Take the gun out now. Hold it in your hand."

Bourne watched helplessly as Fontaine was taken through the door of the church. From the pocket of his jacket there was a sharp sound; the Frenchman's radio had been found and destroyed.

Bourne crawled forward to the two guards and whispered, "They've taken Fontaine inside."

"Where is the other guard?" asked the man near Bourne.

Bourne shook his head. "I'm afraid he may be dead."

Suddenly, there came a long scream, followed by words screamed in pain: "No, no! You are horrible! … Stop, stop!"

"Now!" cried Bourne, as he jumped over the wall. "The lights!" he shouted. "Shoot them out!"

The taller guard's Uzi fired and the lines of lights exploded on both sides of the church's path. Then a single yellow beam appeared, moving quickly in all directions; it was a powerful flashlight in the guard's left hand. The figure of an old man in a brown suit lay curled up on the path, his throat cut.

"*Stop!* In the name of *God*, stop where you are!" came

Fontaine's voice from inside the church, the open door showing the light of electric candles. They approached the entrance, automatic weapons leveled, prepared for continuous fire … but not prepared for what they saw. Bourne closed his eyes—the sight was too painful. Old Fontaine was tied over a table, his face running with blood where he had been cut, and attached to his body were thin cables that led to various black boxes on both sides of the church.

"Go *back*!" screamed Fontaine. "*Run*, you fools! I'm wired."

"Oh, *God!*"

"Don't feel sorry for me. I gladly join my wife! This world is too ugly even for me. *Run*!"

Bourne and the tall guard ran, and fell to the ground.

The explosion was enormous, blinding and deafening. Flames climbed high into the night sky and blew away in the wind.

Then, as their hearing returned to normal, there was the roar of powerful engines as a huge speedboat moved out of a shadowed section of the bay and sped out to sea. The beam of a searchlight shot out, lighting up the barriers of rock rising above the waves. *Carlos!* … The Jackal had changed. He had aged, grown thinner, and lost some hair—he was not the sharp, broad, muscular image of Bourne's memory.

The boat's motors screamed as it reached full speed. Then the words, in heavily accented English, came from the distant loudspeaker.

"*Paris*, Jason Bourne! Paris, if you *dare*!"

Chapter 7 Paris

Steven DeSole, keeper of the deepest secrets for the Central Intelligence Agency, forced his overweight body out of the driver's seat. He stood in the deserted parking lot of the small shopping center in Annapolis, Maryland, where the only source of light came from a closed gas station. DeSole looked at his watch. It was three-thirty in the morning.

The headlights of an approaching limousine shot through the darkness at the far end of the parking lot, turning toward the CIA analyst, causing him to shut his eyes. He had to make the process of his discovery of the information clear to those men. They provided the money that was the means to a life he and his wife dreamed of—education at the best universities for their six grandchildren, not the state colleges that came with the salary of a government worker. The new Medusa had offered money, and he had come running.

Two men got out of the limousine and approached him.

"What does this Webb look like?" asked Albert Armbruster, as they walked along the edge of the parking lot.

"I've only got some old photographs and physical details from his army files," DeSole said. "He's rather large—tall, I mean—and now he'll be in his late forties or early fifties—"

"Can't you be more exact than that?" The other man, short and strong with dark eyebrows beneath dark hair, looked at DeSole. "Be specific," he added.

"Now, just a minute," protested the analyst. "The information I'm giving you is the best I can get and, frankly, whoever you are, I don't like the tone of your voice."

"He's upset," said Armbruster. "He's an Italian from New York and he doesn't trust anybody."

"Who *can* you trust in New York?" asked the short, dark man, laughing.

Armbruster looked at DeSole again. "Does he have gray eyes?" he asked.

"Well, yes, that was in the files."

"It's Cobra," Armbruster said.

"Who?" DeSole said.

"He called himself Cobra, and he knew all about us."

Armbruster and the man from the Mafia climbed back into the limousine.

"Where's the other car?" Armbruster asked.

The Italian looked at his watch. "It's parked less than a kilometer down the road. The driver will pick up DeSole on his way back and stay with him until the time is right."

"But this Cobra—this *Webb*! Why is he coming after us? What does he *want*?"

"There's a connection with that Jackal character, maybe."

"That doesn't make sense. *We* have no connection with the Jackal."

"Why should you?" asked the Mafia man, grinning. "You've got *us*, right?"

"It's a very loose association and don't you forget it … Cobra—*Webb*, whoever he is, we've got to find him! With what he already knew, plus what I told him, he's dangerous!"

"You said Swayne was dangerous. We took care of him. Do you want to discuss a price?"

Armbruster turned and looked at the calm Sicilian face of his companion. "You mean a … contract? On Cobra—on *Webb*?"

♦

"I'll close for six months, change the name, then start advertising in the magazines before reopening," said John St. Jacques to his brother-in-law.

"Meanwhile, it's best to say nothing," said Bourne.

"Well, we have to give some explanation. I've put out a story about a huge gas explosion, but not many people believe it. Of course, to the world outside, an earthquake down here would only get a few lines on an inside page."

"It will pass. People will find something else to talk about. Meanwhile, it's time for me to leave."

"Where are you going?"

"Paris."

"But what can Paris solve?"

"I can find him. I can take him."

"He's got friends over there."

"I've got Jason Bourne," said David Webb. "Lie for me, Johnny. Tell Marie I'm fine and that I have information about the Jackal that only Fontaine could have provided—which is the truth, actually. He told me about a café in Argenteuil called the Soldier's Heart. Call Marie in a couple of hours and bring them back here. It's the safest place they can be."

♦

The next day at ten twenty-five in the morning, Washington time, Dr. Morris Panov, accompanied by his guard, walked out of Walter Reed Hospital after seeing a patient. Panov, thinking about the case, looked at his guard, suddenly surprised.

"You're a new man, aren't you? I mean I thought I knew all of you."

"Yes, sir. We're often sent on short notice."

The psychiatrist continued across the sidewalk to where his car was usually waiting for him. It was a different vehicle.

"This isn't my car," he said, puzzled.

"Get in!" ordered his guard, politely opening the door.

"What?"

A pair of hands from inside the car grabbed him and a uniformed man pulled him into the backseat as the guard followed. The one who had been inside pulled Mo's jacket off his shoulder and pushed up the short sleeve of his summer shirt. He stuck a hypodermic needle into Panov's arm.

"Good night, Doctor," he said. "Call New York," he added, to the guard.

♦

"Mr. Simon?" said the Frenchman, an older man with a small white beard.

"That's right," replied Bourne, shaking hands in a narrow deserted hallway in Paris's Orly Airport.

"I am Bernardine, François Bernardine, an old friend of our friend, Alexander."

"Alex mentioned you," said Bourne, smiling.

"How is he? We hear stories, rumors ... out of Beijing, Hong Kong—some concerning a man named Jason Bourne."

"I've heard them."

"Yes, of course ... But now Paris. Alexander said you would need a place to stay. A hotel?"

"Something small, but I know Montmartre. I'll find a place myself. What I will need is a car—registered under another name, preferably of a dead man."

"It's been arranged; it is in the underground garage on the Capucines, near the Place* Vendôme." Bernardine reached into his pocket, pulled out a set of keys, and handed them to Bourne. "An older Peugeot in Section E. There are thousands of them in Paris and the license number is on the key ring."

"Thank you," said Bourne. "This is very good of you."

"I must explain that I owe my life to Alexander Conklin—and that I know who you are and most of what you have done, Jason Bourne." Bernardine again reached into a pocket and pulled out a card. "Here is my office address—I'm just a consultant now, you understand—and on the back I've written down my home phone. It is a completely secure line. Call me and whatever you need will be provided. Remember, I am

* place: the French word for a square; rue, boulevard, and avenue are French words for street

your only friend in Paris. No one else knows you are here."

Bourne checked into the Pont-Royal on the Rue Montalembert, then walked along the Boulevard Saint-Germain, buying the things he needed. Whatever he could buy now would save time later. Fortunately, there was no need to persuade old Bernardine to supply him with a weapon. During the drive into Paris from Orly, the Frenchman had handed a taped brown box to Bourne. Inside was an automatic with two boxes of bullets. Underneath were 30,000 francs*, around 5,000 American dollars.

"Tomorrow I will arrange a method for you to obtain money whenever necessary. Within limits, of course."

"No limits," Bourne had said. "I'll have Conklin wire you a hundred thousand. Just tell him where."

"Of government money?"

"No. Mine. Thanks for the gun."

Bourne returned to his room and glanced at his watch. It was almost two o'clock, Washington time, and Bernardine had told him that Conklin would be expecting a call. He picked up the phone and called the number in Vienna, Virginia. It was picked up at the first ring.

"Alex, it's me. What happened? Marie—?"

"No," interrupted Conklin. "I spoke to her around noon. She and the kids are back at the hotel and she's ready to kill me. She doesn't believe a word I told her and I'm going to wipe the tape. I haven't heard that kind of language since Vietnam."

"She's upset—"

"So am I," Conklin interrupted. "Mo's disappeared."

"What?"

"You heard me. Panov's gone."

* francs: money used, before euros, in France and Belgium, and still used in Switzerland and some other countries

"My God, how? He's guarded every minute!"

"We're trying to find out."

"But Alex, who? Carlos was on his way back here, to Paris! Whatever he wanted in Washington he got. He found me, he found us. He didn't need any more."

"DeSole's dead," said Conklin quietly. "He knew about me and Mo Panov. I threatened the Agency with both of us, and DeSole was there in the conference room."

"I don't understand. What are you telling me?"

"DeSole was with Medusa. That's why he was killed—to remove our connection."

"To hell with them. I'm not interested in Medusa."

"They're interested in *you*. They want you."

"I couldn't care less. I've only got one priority and he's here."

"Then I haven't been clear," said Conklin, his voice faint. "Last night I had dinner with Mo. I told him everything. Tranquility, your flight to Paris, Bernardine … everything."

♦

On a side street in Anderlecht, five kilometers south of Brussels, a military car with the flags of a general stopped in front of a sidewalk café. General James Teagarten, commander of NATO, stepped out of the car into the early afternoon sunlight. He turned and offered his hand to an attractive female major, who smiled her thanks as she climbed out after him. Teagarten led her across the wide sidewalk toward the café. All the tables were occupied except one at the far end where a small card said *Reserved*.

The owner, with two waiters behind him, came quickly to meet his important guest. When the commander was seated, a bottle of wine was presented and the menu discussed.

A relaxed hour later, Teagarten and his lady were interrupted by the general's driver, a middle-aged army sergeant whose expression showed his anxiety. The commander of NATO had received a message over his secure phone, and the driver had written it down. He handed Teagarten the note.

The general stood up, his sunburned face turning pale as he glanced around the now half-empty café. He reached into his pocket and dropped some Belgian franc notes on the table.

"Come on," he said to the woman major. "Let's go. You"—he turned to his driver—"get the car started!"

"What is it?" asked his lunch companion.

"London. Over the wire. DeSole and Armbruster are dead"

"Oh, my God! How?"

"I don't know. But we're getting out of here. Come *on*!"

The general and his lady rushed across the wide sidewalk and into the military vehicle. The car shot forward, traveling less than fifty meters when it happened.

A great explosion blew the military vehicle into the sky, pieces of glass and metal and lines of blood filling the narrow street in Anderlecht.

Later that afternoon, the waiter in the sidewalk café called to his boss as police, firefighters, and ambulance crews continued their bloody business in the road.

"What is it?" replied the upset owner of the café, still shaking from the hard questioning he had gone through from the police and the journalists. "I am ruined," he said. "We will be known as the café of death."

"Sir, *look*!" The waiter pointed at the table where the general and his lady had sat.

"The police have examined it," said the owner.

Across the glass top of the table, in capital letters written in red lipstick, was a name:

JASON BOURNE.

Chapter 8 The Soldier's Heart

Bourne had moved to a cheaper hotel and changed his appearance. He was wearing faded pants and an old French army shirt. He had a day's growth of beard and his hair and eyebrows were colored red. Out on the street, he knew he had to walk a number of blocks before he found a taxi; taxis were not the fashion in this section of Montparnasse ... Neither was the noisy crowd around a newspaper kiosk at the second corner. People were shouting, many waving their arms, holding newspapers in their fists, anger and puzzlement in their voices. He walked faster, reached the stand, threw down his coins, and grabbed a newspaper.

The breath went out of him as he tried to control the shock waves that swept through him. *Teagarten killed!* The assassin, *Jason Bourne! Madness!* What had *happened?* Was he losing what was left of his *mind*?

He broke away from the crowd and leaned against the stone wall of a building, breathing hard. Alex! A *telephone!*

"What *happened*?" he screamed into the mouthpiece to Vienna, Virginia.

"Calm down," said Conklin quietly. "Where are you? Bernardine will pick you up and get you out. He'll make arrangements and put you on a plane to New York."

"Wait a minute! ... The Jackal did this, didn't he?"

"We've been told that it was a contract from some crazy people in Beirut. That may be true or it may not. But to answer your question, of course it was the Jackal!"

"So he blamed it on me. *Carlos* blamed it on *me!*"

"He's smart, I'll say that for him. You come after him and he uses a contract that keeps you there, hidden, in Paris."

"Then we turn it *around!* While he thinks I'm running and hiding, I'm walking right into his nest."

"You're crazy! You get out while we can still get you out."

"Sorry, Alex, this is exactly where I want to be."

"Well, maybe I can change your mind. I spoke to Marie a couple of hours ago. She's flying to Paris. To find you."

"She *can't!*"

"That's what I said, but she wouldn't listen. She said she knew all the places you and she used thirteen years ago. That you'd use them again. She's on her way."

Bourne put down the phone and walked away.

♦

Morris Panov sat in a chair by a window, looking out over the green fields of a farm somewhere, he assumed, in Maryland. He was in a small second-floor bedroom, his bare right arm confirming what he already knew. He had been drugged repeatedly, his mind emptied, his thoughts and secrets brought chemically to the surface.

The damage he had done was incalculable. He understood that, but what he did not understand was why he was still alive and being treated so well.

The door opened and his guard walked in, a short, well-built man with an accent that Panov placed somewhere in the north-eastern United States. Over his left arm were the psychiatrist's clothes.

"OK, Doc, you have to get dressed. I made sure everything was cleaned and pressed." The guard handed Panov his clothes. "Come on, put them on, Doc, we're going on a little trip."

"I suppose it would be foolish to ask where," said Panov, getting out of the chair.

"Very foolish."

♦

"*Valuable?*" cried the Mafia boss in his living room in Brooklyn

Heights. "Of course, you fool. Panov has worked on the heads of some of the top people in Washington. His files must be worth the price of Detroit."

"You'll never get them, Louis," said the middle-aged man in an expensive suit. "They'll be taken out of your reach."

"Well, we're working on that. Five million is still the price for this Bourne-Webb character, right?" Louis De Fazio said.

"With a condition."

"I don't like conditions, Mr. Lawyer. I don't like them at *all*."

"I don't think you'll be offended."

"Go on."

"There'll be two million dollars extra, because we insist you include Webb's wife and his government friend Conklin."

"Agreed."

"Now, to the rest of the business." He laid an envelope on the table. "This contains payment for Armbruster and Teagarten."

"According to Panov," interrupted the Mafia boss, "they know about two more of you. An ambassador in London and that senior officer in Washington. You want us to take care of them?"

"Possibly later—not now. They both know very little, and nothing about the financial operations. I'll let you know."

Bryce Ogilvie, of the Manhattan law firm Ogilvie, Spofford, Crawford, and Cohen, rose from his seat and left the room.

♦

Morris Panov sat in the front seat of the car with his guard, his hands loosely, almost politely tied, and with a cloth around his eyes. They had been driving for about thirty minutes in silence when the guard spoke.

"You know, Doc, I have a nephew, my sister's kid, who's a doctor, too. I paid for him to go through medical school.

He keeps asking me where the money came from."

"That's very generous of you. But I'm surprised he hasn't said anything about your mouth."

"My mouth? What the hell's wrong with my mouth?"

"The yellow on your teeth, and the fading pink of your gums."

"So? They've always been like that."

"It might be nothing, but he should have spotted it. It could be serious. When did you last see a dentist?"

"I don't like dentists."

"You should see one. You could have problems."

Silence. Then seven minutes later: "What kind of problems?"

"Anything from infection to more serious stuff."

Silence. Four minutes later: "What's the most serious?"

"Mouth cancer. If it's caught in time, it can be stopped with minor bone removal. If not, the entire jaw might have to go."

Panov could feel the car swing to one side as the driver momentarily lost control.

Silence. A minute and a half later: "The whole jaw?"

"It's either that or the whole of the patient's life."

"You think I could have something like that?"

"I'm not a dentist. I can't say for sure."

"You're a doctor, aren't you? I mean you went to medical school?"

"Yes."

"So look at me!"

"I can't. I can't see anything." Panov suddenly felt the guard's thick strong hand pulling the cloth off his head. The car was dark inside. Except for the front window, the windows were almost black.

"Go on, look!" The Mafia man turned his head toward Panov, his thick lips parted and his teeth showing.

"It's too dark in here," replied Mo, seeing what he wanted

to see in the front window; they were on a narrow country road. Wherever he was being taken, he was being driven there by an extremely indirect route.

"Open the window!" shouted the guard, his head still twisted, his eyes still on the road.

Panov lowered the window on his side, seeing nothing but trees and bushes.

"There we are," he continued, raising his loosely tied hands to the Mafia man's mouth—his eyes, however, not on that mouth but on the road ahead. "Oh, my God!" he cried.

"*What?*" screamed the guard.

"Infection—it's everywhere. In the upper and lower jaws. The worst sign."

"Oh, God!"

A huge tree. Up ahead. On the left-hand side of the empty road! Morris Panov put his tied hands on the wheel, lifting his body off the seat as he pushed the wheel to the left. Then at the last second before the car hit the tree, he threw himself to the right, curling up for protection.

The crash was enormous. Broken glass and crushed metal accompanied the rising mists of steam, and the growing fires underneath that would soon reach a gas tank. The guard was still breathing, not dead, his face bleeding. Panov pulled him out of the wreck and into the grass as far as he could, just before the car exploded.

Panov released his loosely tied hands and picked the pieces of glass out of the guard's face. He then checked for broken bones, but it seemed that the man had been lucky. Panov searched the guard's clothing, astonished at the money that was there—about 6,000 dollars—and the various driver's licenses—five different identities from five different states. He took the money and the licenses to give to Alex Conklin, but he left the wallet. There were photographs of the man's family.

Goodbye, my friend, thought Panov, as he crawled over to the road, stood up, and smoothed his clothes, trying to look as respectable as possible. He started to walk, continuing north, in the direction the car had been taking.

♦

The Soldier's Heart was not on a boulevard or an avenue. Instead, it was in a dead-end alley around the corner from a closed factory in what had to be the ugliest part of Argenteuil. Bourne limped through the door and made his way to the crowded bar. He bought a beer and looked around. The place was full of men who looked like soldiers or former soldiers. Fights started from time to time, and were stopped by the muscular waiters.

Bourne took out a piece of paper and wrote on it:

The nest of a blackbird is worth a million francs. Object: private business advice. If interested, be at the old factory around the corner in thirty minutes. Where is the harm? An additional 5,000 francs for being there alone.

Bourne folded the paper over a hundred-franc note and signaled the barman. Slowly, the man moved his large body forward and leaned his thick tattooed arms on the bar.

"What is it?" he asked.

"I have written a message for you," replied Bourne. "I am a man who carries wounds but I'm not a poor man." Bourne passed the paper and the banknote, then turned and headed for the door.

Outside, he hurried up the broken sidewalk toward the alley's entrance. He stood still, moving only his hand to feel the hard steel and the security of his automatic. Ten minutes passed, then fifteen, then the door of the café opened and the barman came out. Bourne watched as he walked across the street.

"I am here," said the barman.

"And I am grateful. Your name?"

"Santos. I believe you mentioned 5,000 francs in your note."

"It's here." Bourne held out the money.

"Thank you," said Santos, walking forward and accepting the bills. "*Take* him!" he added.

Suddenly, Bourne heard running footsteps behind him. Before he could reach his weapon, something heavy crashed down on his head.

Chapter 9 The Blackbird

"We're alone," said the voice across the dark room as Bourne opened his eyes. The barman sat in a large armchair.

Bourne felt the angry swelling on the top of his head.

"There's no break, no blood—only what I imagine is a very painful lump," said the Jackal's man.

"That's accurate, especially the last part."

"At your side, on a table, is an ice bag. You should use it."

Bourne reached down, grabbed the cold bag, and brought it to his head. "You are very kind," he said coldly.

"What do you know about a blackbird?" said the barman.

"Do we do business—a million francs' worth?"

"It seems to me that if a buyer mentions such an amount in the first offer, he will go higher," the Jackal's man said. "A million and a half. Maybe even two."

"But I'm not the buyer, I'm the middleman. I was given permission to pay one million. Take it or leave it. I have other options."

"Do you really?"

"Certainly."

"Not if you're a dead body found floating in the Seine without any identification."

"I see." Bourne looked around the darkened flat. It was very different from the dirty café below. The furniture was tastefully selected—not elegant, but certainly not cheap. Mildly astonishing were the bookshelves covering the wall between the two windows. The academic in Bourne wished he could read the titles; they might give him a clearer picture of this strange, huge man whose speech might have been formed at the Sorbonne*. His eyes returned to the barman. "Then I can't assume I'll leave here alive?"

"No," answered the Jackal's man.

"Of course, you're losing any chance of collecting a million francs—or, as you suggested, maybe a great deal more."

"Then may I suggest," said the barman, crossing his thick arms in front of him as if he were a priest and glancing at the tattoos on his skin, "that a man who has such large available funds will not only part with them in exchange for his life, but will happily deliver the information requested to avoid unnecessary and severe pain." The Jackal's man suddenly shouted, "What do you know about a *blackbird*? Who told you about the Soldier's Heart? Where do you come from and who *are* you and who is your *client*?"

Bourne froze, his body tense but his mind spinning, racing. He had to get out!

"Obviously I don't wish to die for a client or be hurt to protect his information, so I'll tell you what I know, which isn't much. First, the funds are not available to me personally. I meet with a man in London to whom I deliver the information and he releases an account in Bern, Switzerland, to a name and number—any name, any number—that I give him.

"Second, what do I know about a blackbird and the Soldier's Heart? I was told that an old man—I suspect he was French—

* Sorbonne: one of the oldest colleges of the University of Paris

approached a well-known public figure and told him he was the target of an assassination. Who believes a drunk old man? Unfortunately, the assassination took place, but fortunately an assistant to the victim was by his side when the old man warned him. Even more fortunate, the assistant is extremely close to my client and the assassination was a welcome event to both. The assistant secretly passed on the old man's information: a blackbird is sent a message through a café known as the Soldier's Heart in Argenteuil.

"Who am I? My offices are hotel rooms in various cities. I'm currently registered under the name of Simon at the Hotel Pont-Royal, where I keep my passports and other papers." Bourne paused, his open hands outstretched. "I've told you the entire truth as I know it."

"*Not* the entire truth," said the barman. "Who is your client?"

"I'll be killed if I tell you."

"I'll kill you now if you don't!" He picked up Bourne's hunting knife. The blade shone in the light of the floor lamp.

"My client—my clients—are a group of powerful men in the United States. They guard their names like nuclear secrets, but I know of one, and he should be enough for you."

"*Who?*"

"Find out for yourself—find out that I'm telling you the truth, and in the process make yourself so rich that you can do anything you want to do for the rest of your life. Where's the harm? I can be refused, my clients refused. There's no trap. My clients don't want to see the blackbird. They want to *hire* him."

"How could this be done? How can I be satisfied?"

"Invent a high position for yourself and reach the American ambassador in London—the name is Atkinson. Tell him you've received secret instructions from Snake Lady. Ask him if you should accept them."

"Snake Lady? What's that?"

"Medusa. They call themselves Medusa."

♦

"Where the hell *are* you?" shouted Alexander Conklin in Virginia.

"I don't *know,*" Panov replied."They drugged me, Alex. I talked."

"We assumed that. We have to know where you are. Others are looking for you, too."

"A guy in a truck gave me a lift and I jumped off in the first town, but I didn't see a sign. Wait a minute! There's a drugstore across the street. The sign says *Battle Ford's Best.* Will that help?"

There was a sigh on the line. "Yes, if you knew anything about the Civil War, *you'd* know it, too. Find your way to the old battleground at Ford's Bluff. There are signs everywhere. A helicopter will be there in thirty minutes, and don't say anything to anybody!"

♦

Bourne walked into the Hotel Pont-Royal and immediately approached the night concierge, taking out a 500 franc note and placing it quietly in the man's hand.

"The name is Simon," he said, smiling. "I've been away. Any messages?"

"No messages, Mr. Simon," was the quiet reply, "but two men are outside, one on the Montalembert, the other across on the Rue du Bac. They are watching or waiting for somebody."

Bourne removed a thousand-franc note and gave it to the man. "I pay for such eyes and I pay well. Keep watching."

"Of course, sir."

Reaching his room, Bourne saw that everything was as he had left it. The bed. Oh, God, he needed to rest, to sleep.

He couldn't *do* it any longer. Something was happening inside him—less energy, less breath. He wanted to lie down. *No.* There was Marie. There was Bernardine. He went to the telephone and dialed the number.

"Nothing," the old man said. "She is not on any international flight currently in the air or scheduled for departure. I even checked the transfers from London, Lisbon, Stockholm, and Amsterdam—nothing."

"There has to be. She wouldn't change her mind; it's not like her. And she wouldn't know how to avoid Immigration."

"I repeat. She's not listed on any flight from any country coming into Paris."

"Damn."

"I will keep trying, my friend. According to Alex, one should never underestimate your Marie."

♦

François Bernardine woke up suddenly, frowning, disturbed. *She wouldn't change her mind.* The words of the husband who knew her best. *She's not listed on any flight from any country coming into Paris.* His own words. *Paris.* The important word was *Paris!*

But suppose it was *not* Paris?

Bernardine crawled rapidly out of bed in the early morning light. He shaved, washed, dressed, and walked down into the street to his Peugeot. Fifty-eight minutes later, he swung the car into the parking lot of a small plain brick building in Orly Airport. It was a branch of the Department of Immigration, an important one known as the Office of Air Entries, where computers kept up-to-date records of every traveler flying into France at all the international airports.

Nineteen minutes later, he had his answer—but the information was too late. Bernardine found a payphone and dialed the Pont-Royal.

"Yes?" said the voice of Jason Bourne.

"It's François. I apologize for waking you."

"I was just getting up. What's happening?"

"I'm out at Orly and I'm afraid I have bad news. Your wife flew into Marseilles slightly over two hours ago. Not Paris. Marseilles."

"Why is that bad news? cried Bourne. "We know where she is! We can—oh God, I see what you mean … She can take a train, hire a car. "

"She can even fly up to Paris under any name she wants to use."

♦

Bourne's watch read one o'clock when two men walked out of the alley and across the street.

"Santos will see you now," said one of them.

"I don't see him."

"You have to come with us. He does not leave the Soldier's Heart."

"Why do I not like that?"

"There is no reason for such feelings. As I said earlier, he has peace in his heart."

Bourne was led down the alley, past the café's entrance, to a small break in the buildings. One by one, Bourne between the two men, they made their way to the back of the café. Bourne was led, through an unexpectedly beautiful garden, to a small outside elevator. It barely held the three of them. When the iron gate was closed, the silent messenger pressed a button in the darkness and spoke.

"We are here, Santos. Camellia. Bring us up."

"Camellia?" asked Bourne.

"He knows everything is all right," said the other man. "If not, my friend might have said 'rose.'"

"What would happen then?"

"You don't want to think about it."

The elevator stopped and the quiet messenger opened a thick, steel door. Bourne was led into the familiar room with its tasteful, expensive furniture.

"You may leave, my friends," said Santos from an armchair.

The two messengers, instead of heading for the back of the room and the elevator, opened a door in the left wall and disappeared.

"Sit down, Mr. Simon," said Santos. "How is your head?"

"The swelling's gone down, thank you." Bourne sat on the large couch. "I understand you have peace in your heart."

"And a desire for three million francs."

"Then you were satisfied with your call to London?"

"Yes. No one could have programmed the ambassador into reacting the way he did. He was very frightened. There *is* a Snake Lady and she creates extraordinary fear in high places. Now, you say that you and you *alone* must reach the blackbird. May I ask why?"

"Because if one drunk old man can talk about the Soldier's Heart, then others may do so. You can be traced by the police. My clients want no connection with you."

"Even through you?"

"Later, I'll disappear. You won't—though maybe you should think about doing so. Here, I brought you something." Bourne sat forward on the couch and reached into his back pocket. He pulled out a roll of franc notes held together by a rubber band. He threw it over to Santos, who caught it in mid-air. "200,000 francs in advance. Give me the information I need and I'll deliver it to London. Whether or not the blackbird accepts my clients' offer, you will still receive the balance of the three million."

Santos got up from the chair and walked across to a card table.

"If you will, please come over here."

Bourne rose from the couch and walked over to the card table, suddenly astonished. Spread across the table were his three passports, as well as the gun and the knife taken from him last night.

"I'll accept your money now," said Santos, "but instead of you flying to London, London will fly to Paris. Tomorrow morning. When he arrives at the Pont-Royal, you'll call me—I'll give you my private number, of course. Then we'll have an exchange: the money for the information."

"I'll do what I can," said Bourne.

♦

Two hours later, he called Bernardine.

"My God, it is four o'clock in the morning, so I can assume you have something important to tell this seventy-year-old man."

"I've got a problem."

"You've got too many problems, but never mind. What is it?"

"I'm as close as I can be, but I need another man."

"What kind of man?"

"My contact with the Jackal expects an Englishman to fly over from London this morning with two million, eight hundred thousand francs "

"Far less money than you have, I assume."

"Yes, but I'm being watched, so I can't go to the bank, and I don't have an Englishman to bring what I can't get to the Pont-Royal."

"I can get the money for you. Sign a paper releasing it to me. Give the paper to the hotel concierge and I'll pick it up."

"Fine. What about the Englishman? This morning?"

"Not a problem, old boy!" said the Frenchman in a perfect English accent.

Soon after four-thirty in the afternoon, Bernardine walked into the Pont-Royal dressed in a dark suit that was obviously British. He went to the elevator and eventually, after two wrong turns, reached Bourne's room.

"Here's the money," he said, dropping a small case on the floor. He sat down at the desk, took two automatics and three grenades from his pockets, and placed them in a row. "I will relax now."

"What the hell is *that*—are *they?*" cried Bourne.

"When you go out to do your business, you will leave the door open," replied Bernardine. "If somebody comes down that narrow passage, he will see a grenade in my hand."

"That makes sense," said Bourne, going to the door.

Out on the Montalembert, he walked to the corner, leaned against the wall, and waited.

A man walked across the street toward him. It was the talkative messenger from last night, his hand in his jacket pocket.

"Where's the money?"

"Where's the information?" answered Bourne.

"The money first."

"That's not the arrangement." Without warning, Bourne grabbed him by the jacket, pulling him forward off his feet. Bourne moved up his free hand and gripped the messenger's throat, his fingers digging into the man's flesh. "You go back to Santos and tell him he's got a one-way ticket to hell. I don't *deal* this way."

"*Enough!*" said the low voice, its owner coming around the corner on Bourne's right. The huge figure of Santos approached. "Let him go, Simon. He is nothing. It is now only you and me."

Bourne released the messenger, who looked at Santos. Responding to a gesture of his boss's large head, the man raced away.

"Your Englishman arrived," said Santos when they were

alone. "He carried a small case. I saw myself. So I shall give you the information. What I am going to tell you, Mr. Simon, is known by only four people in the world. However, if you even hint at Argenteuil as your source of information, I'll know it immediately and you will never leave the Pont-Royal alive."

"The contact can be made so quickly?"

"With a telephone number. But you will not place the call for at least an hour from the moment we part. If you do, again I will know it, and again, I tell you, you're a dead man."

"An hour. Agreed. Only three other people have this number? Why not choose one that you're not particularly fond of so that I can mention him—if it's necessary?"

Santos smiled thinly. "Moscow," he said softly. "High up in Dzerzhinsky Square."

"The *KGB?*"

"The blackbird is building a network in Moscow. Always Moscow—he's fascinated by it."

Ilich Ramirez Sanchez, thought Bourne. Trained at Novgorod. Dismissed by the KGB as a madman. The Jackal!

"I'll remember that—if it's needed. The number, please?"

Santos said it twice, with the words that Bourne had to say. He spoke slowly, obviously impressed that Bourne wrote nothing down. "Is that all clear?"

"Yes," said Bourne. "If everything goes as I hope it will, how do you want me to get you the money?"

"Call me—you've got my number. I will leave Argenteuil and come to you. And never return to Argenteuil."

"Good luck, Santos. Something tells me you deserve it."

"No one more so. Goodbye."

Santos walked away and Bourne, his heart beating fast, headed back to the Pont-Royal.

"Bernardine!" he said, entering his room. "Put the weapons away. We've struck gold."

"In what way?"

"An hour," announced Bourne. "Forty-three minutes from now. Write this down, François." Bourne repeated the phone number given to him by Santos. "Can you find out where that number is?"

"It might take some time and cost money—"

"The money doesn't matter—and I'll pay more for less time."

Bernardine picked up the phone.

♦

Former judge Bernard Prefontaine watched Randolph Gates cry as the professor sat forward on the couch in Boston's Ritz-Carlton Hotel, his face in his hands.

"So you got into trouble in France, Randy?"

"My *God*, how did you find out?"

"You know I can't possibly tell you that. But these things leave a trace."

The trace, in this case, was a file held by Army Intelligence. Conklin had found a reference to it in Swayne's diary and asked Casset to investigate.

"You don't know what it was *like*!" said Gates. "I was setting up a business deal when I was kidnapped. Then I was thrown into a plane and flown to Marseilles, where the most horrible things happened to me. I was kept in a room and every few hours I was given drugs—for more than six weeks. Women were brought in, movies made—I wasn't myself."

"So you became the Jackal's man in the world of high finance?"

"It's how he found me. The deal I was trying to do was opposed by some people in the Far East. They hired him ... Oh, my God, he'll *kill* me!"

"Yes, he probably will. Sorry about that, Randy."

"What am I going to *do*?"

"There's a way. First, a long rest at a private health center—but even before that, your complete cooperation right now. If you help, the Jackal will be killed, and you'll be free, Randy."

"I'll do *anything*!"

"How do you reach him?"

"I have a telephone number!" Gates took his wallet from his pocket and dug into it with trembling fingers. "Only four people alive have it!"

♦

The hour was over, and Bourne left the hotel, walking slowly, crossing four streets until he saw a public phone by the River Seine. It was dark now and the boats on the river were dotted with lights. He breathed steadily, controlling himself, as he went inside, put in a coin, and dialed.

"Yes?" It was a woman's voice.

"Blackbirds circle in the sky," said Bourne, repeating Santos's words in French. "They make a great deal of noise but one is silent."

A man's voice came on the line. "Who is this?" The *Jackal!* It *was* the Jackal! The smooth, fast French could not hide the Latin American accent.

"Somebody who was trusted by somebody who knows you with this number. I can offer you the contract of your career, of your *life*. You can name your price, but those who pay are among the most powerful men in the United States."

"This is a very strange call. Very unusual."

"All I need is your interest at this point. If the answer is yes, I can reveal more. If it's no, well, I tried, but I am forced to go elsewhere. The newspapers say he was in Brussels only yesterday. I'll find him." There was a sharp intake of breath at the mention of Brussels, and the unspoken name of Jason

Bourne. "Yes or no, blackbird?"

Silence. Finally the Jackal spoke. "Call me back in two hours," he ordered, hanging up the phone.

It was *done!* Bourne leaned against the pay phone, the sweat pouring down his face and breaking out on his neck. The Pont-Royal. He had to get back to Bernardine!

"It was Carlos!" he announced, closing the door and crossing to the bedside phone while taking Santos's card out of his pocket. He dialed. Seconds later, he spoke. "The bird's confirmed," he said. "Give me a name, any name." The pause was brief. "The case will be left with the concierge. Send one of your men. If he uses that name the concierge will give it to him. Count the money and send my passports back to me."

Bourne hung up and turned to Bernardine.

"We have an address on the Boulevard Lefébvre for that phone," the Frenchman said, and told Bourne the number.

"I'm leaving," said Jason Bourne, taking Bernardine's automatic off the desk and putting two grenades in his pocket. "Do you mind?"

"Take them," replied the Frenchman, pulling another gun from his belt. "But why?"

"I've got at least a couple of hours and I want to look around."

"*Alone?*"

"How else? If we call for support, I risk being gunned down or spending the rest of my life in jail for an assassination I was not involved with in Belgium."

♦

Bernardine stared at the ringing telephone, wondering whether to pick it up. He had to.

"Yes?"

"Jason? It's you, isn't it? Maybe I have the wrong room."

"Alex? This is you?

"François? What are you doing there? Where's Jason?

"Things have happened so fast. I know he's been trying to reach you."

"It's been a difficult day. We've got Panov back."

"That's good news."

"I've got other news. A telephone number where the Jackal can be reached."

"We've got it! And an address. Our man left an hour ago."

"For God's sake, how did you *get* it?"

"A complex process that I believe only your man could have handled. He's very imaginative."

"Let's compare," said Conklin. "What's yours."

Bernardine said the number he had written down on Bourne's instructions.

The silence on the phone was a silent scream, "They're different,' said Conklin finally. "They're *different!*"

"A trap," said Bernardine. "God, it's a *trap!*"

Chapter 10 The Meurice

Twice, Bourne had passed the dark, quiet row of old stone houses on the Boulevard Lefébvre. He then returned to the Rue d'Alésia and found a sidewalk café. He ordered coffee.

As the waiter returned to the service bar, Bourne pulled out his small notebook and pen, shutting his eyes for a moment, then opening them and drawing everything he could remember. There were three pairs of attached houses separated by narrow alleys. Each double complex was three floors high, each front entrance reached by climbing a steep flight of brick steps. At either end of the row were vacant lots. The address of the Jackal's telephone number was the final structure on the right, though maybe he occupied the whole row.

Bourne left the café and walked slowly, as an older man might walk, toward the Boulevard Lefébvre. The closer he came to the last corner, the more he became aware of the rising and falling sounds from different directions. *Police cars!* What had happened? Bourne ran to the edge of the building in front of the Lefébvre. What were they doing?

Five police cars arrived from different directions, each stopping in front of the building on the right. Then a large police van appeared, its searchlight shooting out as a group of black-uniformed men with automatic weapons leaped out into the street and crouched behind the police cars.

Fools. To give Carlos a warning was to lose the Jackal! Killing was his profession and escape was part of it. For God's sake, who had *done* this?

"On police authority, all residents will leave the building." The orders came over a loudspeaker and echoed down the street. *"You have one minute before we break into the house."*

The door above the flight of brick steps on the right opened, and a nun dressed in black appeared.

"How *dare* you? she roared. "This is the evening prayer time and you disturb us. You should be asking forgiveness for your sins, not interrupting those who beg *God* to forgive theirs!"

"Nicely said, Sister," said the voice over the loudspeaker. "But we have other information and we insist on searching your house."

He knew that voice! It was Bernardine! What had happened! Was Bernardine his enemy after all? Was it all an act?

The black-uniformed group raced to the base of the brick steps. An official in plain clothes, the obvious leader of the assault, joined his unit on the sidewalk below the steps. Then he and his men raced up the brick stairs through the door held open by the angry nun.

Bourne held his place at the edge of the building, his eyes on the strange scene on Lefébvre. Twelve minutes passed, then the assault team left, several members bowing and kissing the hand of the real or pretending nun.

"*Bernardine!*" screamed the official, approaching the first police car. "You are finished! *Out!* Never are you to talk to anybody in the Deuxième* again! If I had my way, you'd be shot! *Nuns!* Get out of my car before I shoot you by accident!"

Bernardine got out of the police car, his old unsteady legs barely able to maintain balance. The police cars and the van raced away. Bourne had to wait, his eyes moving from Bernardine to the front entrance of the Jackal's house. And it *was* the Jackal's house; the nun proved it. Carlos could never let go of his lost faith. He often used it as cover, but it was much more than that. Much more.

Bernardine walked into the shadows of a storefront across from the house of the nuns. Bourne reached the corner and ran down the sidewalk.

"For God's sake, what *happened*?" he cried.

"It's a trap, my friend," said Bernardine.

"*What*?"

"Alex and I confirmed it. The telephone numbers were different. I gather that you didn't make your call to Carlos."

"No. I had the address and I wanted him to wait. What's the difference? This is the *house*!"

"Oh, this is where your Mr. *Simon* was supposed to go, and if he was truly *Mr. Simon* he would be taken to another place. But if he was not Mr. Simon but somebody else, then he would be shot—bang—another dead body in search of the Jackal."

"You're *wrong*!" insisted Bourne. "Carlos isn't going to allow anybody to kill me except himself. Those are his orders."

He hid, watched, and waited.

* Deuxième: the French intelligence service

At five-seventeen, two bicycles ridden by nuns stopped in front of the house. The door opened and three more nuns, each carrying a bicycle, walked out and down the brick steps to join them. They started up the street, Carlos's nun behind the others. Bourne moved out from the storefront and ran after them.

At an intersection of the Rue Lecourbe in Montparnasse, a number of trucks prevented Carlos's nun from keeping up with the others. She waved them on and turned into a narrow side street, suddenly moving faster than before. Bourne did not have to increase his speed. A sign on the building fronting the street said DEAD END. There was no other way out.

He found the bicycle chained to a street lamp and waited in the darkness of a doorway. He leaned against the stone, breathing heavily, feeling the tiredness in his legs. Only a few short years ago there would have been none.

The sound of a handle turning broke the stillness of the street, followed by the noise of a heavy door being opened. It was the entrance to the apartment in front of the chained bicycle. Bourne watched the woman rush to the lamp-post. He walked forward.

"You'll be late for prayers," he said.

The woman spun around. Bourne gripped her arm with his left hand and tore off her large white hat with his right. The sight of the face in front of him came as a shock.

"My God," he whispered. "I *know* you! Paris ... years ago ... your name is Lavier ... Jacqueline *Lavier.* You had one of those dress shops ... Les Classiques. A contact point for Carlos in the Faubourg. I thought you were *dead.*"

The woman's sharp, middle-aged face twisted in anger. She tried to break out of his grip, but Bourne crashed her against the wall.

"You're wrong!" said the woman, her green eyes wide. It's true, I am Lavier. But I'm not the woman you knew. You knew my sister, Jacqueline—I am *Dominique* Lavier. We were close in age and looked very like each other, Jason Bourne."

"You know who I am?"

"All Paris—the Jackal's Paris—knows who you are. Not by sight, but they know you are here and they know you're tracking Carlos."

"And you're part of that Paris?"

"I am."

"Good God, lady, he killed your *sister*!"

"She knew the rules. She betrayed him. And at my age, my choices are limited. I took Jacqui's place at Les Classiques."

"Just like that?"

"It wasn't difficult. Jacqui supposedly went to Switzerland for some work on her face … and I returned to Paris after eight weeks of preparation."

"And went into the killing game."

"I was gradually led into it. In the beginning, I was told that Jacqueline had died in a boating accident and that I would be well paid to carry on in her place. By the time I found out the truth … well, he was paying me well and I was afraid of him."

"It's all an old story," said Bourne. "This is now, thirteen years later. What happens now?"

"I don't know. My choices are zero, aren't they? One or the other of you will kill me, I suppose."

"Maybe not. Help me take him and you're free of both of us. You can go to the Mediterranean and live in peace—and comfort. Carlos can't reach you because he'll be dead."

"And does this comfort come from you?"

"Yes."

"I see … Is that what you offered Santos? A comfortable disappearance?"

Bourne looked at his prisoner. "So it was Santos after all," he said softly. "Lefébvre *was* a trap. God, the Jackal's smart."

"Santos is dead. The Soldier's Heart is closed down."

"What?" Stunned, Bourne stared again at the Lavier woman. "That was his reward for trapping me?"

"No, for betraying Carlos."

"I don't understand."

"Carlos's eyes and ears are everywhere. Santos was observed sending several heavy boxes out with his main food supplier. A man was sent to the supplier and opened the boxes."

"Books," interrupted Bourne quietly.

"And he will kill me, too. He will know I have spoken to you." She looked around. "He has eyes everywhere. I am not important to him. I can tell the authorities nothing of substance because I have never seen him. But he will still kill me."

"I see." Bourne stepped back from his prisoner. "I can get you out," he said quietly. "Out of Paris, out of Europe. Beyond Carlos's reach. Do you want that?"

"As eagerly as Santos did," answered Lavier. "I will willingly trade my loyalty from him to you."

"Why?"

"Because he is old and gray-faced and is not as good as you. You offer me life, he offers death."

"That's a reasonable decision, then," said Bourne. "Do you have any money? With you, I mean?"

"I have several hundred francs. Why?"

"It's not enough," continued Bourne, reaching into his pocket and taking out a roll of franc notes. "Here's 3,000" he said, handing her the money. "Buy some clothes somewhere— I'm sure you know how—and take a room at the … the Meurice Hotel on the Rue de Tivoli."

"What name should I use?"

"What suits you?"

"How about Brielle? A lovely town beside the sea."

"Why not? … Give me ten minutes to get out of here and

then leave. I'll see you at the Meurice at noon."

"With all my heart, Jason Bourne!"

"Let's forget the name."

Bourne walked out of the dead-end street and went to the nearest taxi station. Within minutes a happy taxi driver accepted a hundred francs to wait in place at the end of the line, his passenger sitting low in the back seat waiting to hear the words.

"The nun comes out, sir!" cried the driver. "She enters the first taxi!"

"Follow it," said Bourne, sitting up.

On the Avenue Victor Hugo, Lavier's taxi slowed down and stopped in front of a public phone.

"Stop here," ordered Bourne, climbing out the moment the driver swung into the side of the street. Bourne walked quickly, silently, to the telephone, behind the nun. He could hear her clearly as he stood three meters away.

"The Meurice!" she shouted into the phone. "The name is Brielle. He'll be there at noon ... Yes, yes, I'll stop at my apartment, change clothes, and be there in an hour." Lavier hung up and turned, shocked by the sight of Bourne. "No!" she screamed.

"Yes, I'm afraid," said Bourne. "'He's old and gray-faced'—those were your words, Dominique. Quite descriptive for somebody who never met Carlos."

A little later an angry Bernardine walked out of the Hotel Pont-Royal and approached the taxi.

"This is mad," he said.

"Get in," said Bourne, on the far side of the woman dressed as a nun. Bernadine did so, staring at her. "Meet one of the Jackal's more talented performers."

The taxi made a U-turn and entered the Rue du Bac. "We're going to the Meurice," added Bourne.

"I'm sure there's a reason," stated Bernardine.

"It's the Jackal's final trap for me," answered Bourne, "thanks to the persuasive lady here. He expects me to be there and I'll be there."

"I'll call in the Deuxième. I still have some friends there."

"No," said Bourne. "I can't take the chance. One man could send out an alarm."

"Let me help," said Dominique Lavier. "I *can* help."

"I listened to your help before, lady, and it was leading me to my own death. No thanks."

"That was before, not now. This old man mentions that he'll call in the Deuxième—the *Deuxième*, Mr. Bourne. Even if I survived, I'd no doubt be sent to some horrible prison halfway across the world—oh, I've heard stories of the Deuxième! Besides," continued Lavier, looking at Bourne, "without me in different clothing at the Meurice, Carlos won't come near it."

"She's right," said Bourne, leaning forward and looking past Lavier at Bernardine. "I think we can trust her now. She's got an apartment on the Montaigne. She can change clothes there."

After a short period of silence, Bernardine spoke. "What's your address on the Avenue Montaigne?"

♦

Marie sat at the table in her small suite at the Meurice Hotel reading the newspapers, but concentration was out of the question. Her anxiety had kept her awake after she returned to the hotel soon after midnight, having visited five cafés she and David had used so many years ago in Paris. Finally, after four in the morning, exhaustion had allowed her to sleep. Now she knew she had to go out again, to keep looking for David.

She put down her coffee cup, picked up her coat, and left the room. The ride down to the ground floor seemed to last forever because of an American couple who kept complaining that not enough people in Paris spoke English. Finally, the elevator doors opened and Marie walked rapidly out into the crowded Meurice hallway.

As she crossed the floor toward the entrance, she suddenly stopped as an elderly man in a dark suit sat straight up in a heavy leather chair on her right. He stared at her, his eyes wide open in shock.

"Marie St. Jacques!" he whispered. "My *God*, get *out* of here!"

"I beg your … *What?*"

The old Frenchman quickly, with difficulty, rose to his feet.

"You cannot be seen here, Mrs. Webb," he said, his voice in a whisper. "Don't look at me! Look at your watch. Keep your head down." The retired Deuxième officer glanced away, his lips barely moving. "Go out of the door on the far left. *Hurry!*"

"No!" replied Marie. "You know me but I don't know you! Who are you?"

"A friend of your husband."

"My God, is he *here*?"

"The question is why are *you* here?

"I stayed at this hotel once before. I thought he might remember it."

"He did, but in the wrong way, I'm afraid. Now *leave*."

"I won't! I have to find him. Where *is* he?"

"You will leave or you may find only his dead body. You cannot do this to him. You'll kill him! Get out of here. *Now!*"

Her eyes half-blinded with anger and with tears, Marie started toward the left side of the door. What could she do—what *should* she do? David was somewhere in the hotel.

Help me! For God's sake, Jason, tell me what to do. Jason? *Yes, Jason* help *me!* Out in the street she stood frozen, as taxis and limousines broke off from the traffic and pulled up beside the Meurice. A large black limousine with a small religious badge on its passenger door moved to a stop. Both doors beside the sidewalk were opened by the doorman as five priests got out, one from the front seat, four from the large back section. The last four priests immediately moved through the crowds to stand two at the front of the vehicle, two at the back.

Suddenly, Marie saw a figure crossing the Rue de Rivoli. It was a tall man in dark clothes and he was limping, avoiding the traffic, but the limp was *false!* The leg straightened, if only for a moment. It was David!

Another, no more than two meters from her, also saw what she saw. A small radio was immediately brought to the man's lips.

"*David!*" Marie screamed.

Gunshots filled the Rue de Rivoli. The crowds panicked, many running into the hotel, many more racing away. The old Frenchman who had recognized her came crashing out of the front entrance, firing into the black limousine.

"*My friend!*" roared Bernardine.

"*Here!*" shouted Bourne, "Where *is* she?"

"*To your right. Next to*—" A single gunshot exploded from the glass double doors of the Meurice. Bernardine fell to the sidewalk. A second gunshot ended his life.

Marie could not *move*! Crying, out of control, she fell to her knees, then onto the street.

"We're getting out of here. Can you understand that?" said Jason Bourne, his voice not the voice of David Webb.

"Yes, yes!" Marie awkwardly got to her feet, held by the husband she either knew or did not know.

"Let's *go!* Bernardine gave us our exit. Run with me; hold my hand!"

Chapter 11 The KGB

Bourne and Marie drove south to the small city of Corbeil-Essonnes, where there was a new shopping center several kilometers west of the highway. From a public telephone Bourne placed a call to Vienna, Virginia, but Alex Conklin wasn't there. Instead, there was the voice of a recorded operator saying, "The telephone number you have called is no longer in service."

Bourne called the apartment in Washington and heard another recorded voice. "This is Alex," it said. "I'll be away for some time, visiting a place where a grave error was made. Call me in five or six hours. It's now nine-thirty in the morning, Eastern Standard Time. Out, Juliet."

Stunned, his mind spinning, Bourne hung up the phone and stared at Marie. "Something's happened and I have to make sense of it. His last words were—"Out, Juliet."

"*Juliet?*" Marie said. "Hotel, India, Juliet—it's the international radio operators' alphabet. Juliet's for J and J is for *Jason*! … What was the rest?"

"He's visiting somewhere 'where a grave error was made'."

"A *what*?"

"He said to call him in five or six hours—he was visiting a place where a grave error—grave?—my God, it's *Rambouillet*!"

"The cemetery …?"

"Where he tried to kill me thirteen years ago—when he thought I'd changed sides. That's *it*! Rambouillet!"

"Not in five or six hours," objected Marie. "Whenever he left the message, he couldn't fly to Paris and then drive to Rambouillet in five hours. He was in Washington."

"Of course he could; we've both done it before. An army jet out of Andrews Air Force Base to Paris." Bourne suddenly looked at his watch. "It's still only around noon in the islands. Let's find another phone."

"Johnny? Tranquility? You really think—"

"I can't stop thinking!" interrupted Bourne, rushing ahead. "There's a phone inside, over there," he said, approaching the huge windows of an ice cream shop. "Get me a chocolate one," he said, leading Marie into the crowded store.

Bourne crossed to the phone, immediately understanding why it was not used; the noise of the store was almost unbearable. Three minutes later, holding his hand against his left ear, Bourne had the unexpected comfort of hearing Tranquility Hotel's most annoying employee over the phone.

"This is Mr. Pritchard, Tranquility Hotel's assistant manager. May I inquire as to the nature of your—"

"You can shut *up*!" shouted Bourne. "Get Johnny St. Jacques on the phone, now. This is his brother-in-law."

"Of course, sir. One moment, please."

"*Johnny*?"

"David, where *are* you?"

"That doesn't matter. Get out of there. Take the kids and Mrs. Cooper and get *out!*"

"We know all about it. Alex Conklin called several hours ago and said somebody named Holland would reach us ... I gather he's the chief of your intelligence service."

"He is. Did he?"

"Yeah, about twenty minutes after I talked to Alex. He told us we're being taken out by helicopter around two o'clock this afternoon. David, what the hell is going on? Where's *Marie*?"

"She's all right—I'll explain everything later. Just do as Holland says. Did he say where you were being taken?"

"He didn't want to, but no American is going to order me and your kids around—my *Canadian* sister's kids. He said we were going to a safe house in Virginia. It's on a piece of land in Fairfax with no public entry and its own airfield."

"I know the place," said Bourne. "It's called Tannenbaum. He's right—it's the best of the safe houses. He likes us."

"I asked you before—where's Marie?"

"She's with me."

"She *found* you!"

"Later, Johnny. I'll reach you in Fairfax." Bourne hung up the phone.

♦

They met at Rambouillet and drove to a small country restaurant: Alex Conklin, Mo Panov, Jason Bourne, and Marie Webb. The family was together. They sat around a table at the back. The owner said that the cooking was extraordinary, but since nobody was hungry Bourne paid for four starters to keep the owner happy.

"We'll be working with the Soviets," Conklin said. "It's all right—Holland arranged it and I know the contact. I've known him for years, but Washington doesn't know that I know him. His name is Krupkin, Dimitri Krupkin, and he can be bought and paid for."

"For how much?" Marie asked.

"Considering his position in the Paris KGB, I'd say around 50,000 American dollars."

"Offer him thirty-five," Marie said, "and go up to seventy-five under pressure. Up to a hundred if necessary, of course."

"For God's *sake*," cried Bourne. "We're talking about *us*, about the *Jackal*. Give him anything he wants! We have the *money*."

"Too easily bought by us, too easily bought by the other side."

"Is she right?" asked Bourne, staring at Conklin.

"Normally, of course, but in this case it would have to be something like a diamond mine. Nobody wants Carlos in the 'dead' file more than the Soviets, and the man who brings in his dead body will be the hero of the Kremlin. Remember, Carlos was trained at Novgorod. Moscow never forgets that."

"Then do as she says— buy him," said Bourne.

"I understand." Conklin leaned forward. "I'll call him tonight, pay phone to pay phone, and get it settled. Then I'll arrange a meeting tomorrow, maybe lunch somewhere outside Paris."

"Why not here?" asked Bourne. "It's quiet and I'll know how to get here."

"Why not?" agreed Conklin. "I'll talk to the owner." He turned to the others. "But not the four of us—just Jason and me."

"I assumed that," said Bourne coldly. "Marie must not be involved. She must not be seen or heard, is that clear?"

"David," said Marie angrily, "you cannot and will not order me around. Do you understand *that*?"

"Loud and clear, lady. Then maybe you should go back to the States so you won't have to listen to me." Jason Bourne rose from the table, pushing the chair behind him. "Tomorrow's going to be a busy day, so I have to get some sleep. I'll be in the car for two minutes. You decide whether to stay or go. I'm sure Alex can get you out of France." Bourne turned and walked away.

"Go to him," said Panov quickly. "You know what's happening."

"I can't *handle* it, Mo!"

"Don't handle it, just be with him. You're the only support he's got. You don't even have to talk, just be there. With him."

"He's become the killer again."

"Then provide him with that link to David Webb. It *has* to be there, Marie."

"Oh, God, I love him so much!" cried the wife, rushing to her feet and racing after the man who was her husband but not her husband.

"Was that the right advice, Mo?" asked Conklin.

"I don't know, Alex. I just don't think he should be alone with his terrors. None of us should. That's not psychiatry, it's just common sense."

"Sometimes you sound like a real doctor—you know that?"

♦

The Algerian section of Paris lies between the tenth and eleventh districts, barely three blocks, where the low buildings are Parisian but the sounds and the smells are Arabic. A long black limousine entered this district, the badge of the Roman Catholic church in gold on the doors. It stopped in front of a wood-framed three-floor house, where an old priest got out and walked to the door. He pressed a button that rang a bell on the second floor.

"Yes?" said the metallic voice from upstairs.

"I am a messenger from the American embassy," answered the visitor. "I can't leave my vehicle, but we have an urgent message for you."

"I'll be right down," said the French-Algerian driver, who worked for the Americans. Three minutes later, the man came out of the building. "What are you dressed like that for?" he asked the messenger, who stood by the large car, covering the badge on the door.

"I'm the embassy's Catholic priest, my son. A member of staff would like a word with you." He opened the car door.

"Yes sir, what can I do for you?" said the driver, as he bent down to look inside the limousine.

"Where did you take our people?" asked the shadowed figure in the darkness.

"What people?" said the Algerian, concern in his voice.

"The two you picked up at the airport several hours ago. The limping man and his friend."

"If you're from the embassy and they want you to know, they'll call and tell you, won't they?"

"*You'll* tell me!"

A third, powerfully built man in a driver's uniform appeared from behind the trunk of the car. He walked rapidly forward, raising his arm and crashing a stick down on the Algerian's head. He pushed his victim inside. The old man dressed as a priest climbed in behind him, pulling the door shut as the driver ran around to the front seat. The limousine raced away.

An hour later, on the deserted Rue Houdon, the Algerian's bruised and bleeding dead body was pushed out of the large car. Inside, the figure in shadows addressed the priest.

"Get your car and remain outside the limping one's hotel. Report any movements and go where he goes. Don't fail me."

"Never, sir."

♦

Dimitri Krupkin was seated at a table in the country restaurant, staring across the table at Alex Conklin, who sat beside the unidentified Bourne.

"So, my dear old enemy," Krupkin said, "how and where will I be paid according to our agreement last night on the telephone?"

"How and where do you *want* to be paid?" asked Bourne.

"Ah ha, *you* are my employer, sir?"

"I'll be paying you, yes."

"I shall write down the name of a bank and the number of an account in Geneva," the Soviet said. He reached into his pocket for a pen, but was not able to use it because a man in his early thirties walked rapidly up to the table.

"What is it, Sergei?" asked Krupkin.

"You have been followed. An old man in a gray car—he arrived soon after you did—looked at the name of the restaurant, then used the car telephone."

"That old man's from the Jackal—" said Bourne.

"Carlos!" cried Krupkin, his blue eyes angry. "The Jackal's after *you*, Aleksei?"

"No, him," answered Conklin, pointing at Bourne.

"Good God! With what we've learned in Moscow, it's all making sense. So I have the honor to meet the famous Jason

Bourne. A great *pleasure*, sir! We have the same aim where Carlos is concerned, do we not?"

"If your men are good, we may achieve that aim before the end of the next hour. Let's get out of here and use the back way, the kitchen. He's found me and you can bet he's coming out here for me. But he doesn't know that we know that. Let's *go*!"

As the three men rose from the table, Krupkin gave instructions to his assistant. "Have the car brought around to the back, Sergei."

"Of course, comrade." The assistant hurried back to the entrance.

They left through the kitchen and waited in Krupkin's Citroen on the edge of a field. Suddenly, a dark brown limousine shot up the road from the highway to Paris. It pulled to a stop in front of the restaurant and two men leaped out of the side door, their faces covered, their hands holding automatic weapons. A third man came out of the vehicle, wearing a priest's black clothing. Suddenly, there was an ear-splitting scream of revenge from the Jackal as the terrorists rushed inside, their weapons on automatic fire.

"Now!" cried Sergei. The Citroen swung out on the road, rushing toward the limousine, but in a split second its progress was stopped. A huge explosion took place on the right. The old man—the informer—and the gray car in which he was sitting were blown up, sending the Citroen to the left into a fence.

"Get out!" shouted Sergei, pulling Bourne from the seat onto the dirt by the fence, as his stunned superior and Alex Conklin crawled out behind him.

"Let's *go*!" cried Bourne. "He blew up the car."

They ran to the front doors of the restaurant and burst inside. The next sixty seconds were like a scene from hell. The waiter and two male customers were dead, lying on the floor with blood running from their heads. Women screamed.

Sergei suddenly rushed forward, his weapon on automatic fire. In a back corner of the room he had spotted a figure whom Bourne had not seen. The killer leaped out of the shadows and the Soviet shot him. But it was *not* Carlos. Where was the *Jackal*?

"In *there!*" shouted Sergei, pointing to the kitchen.

Both men moved toward the swinging doors, but were partially blown back by an explosion from within. A grenade had been thrown. The smoke blew out into the dining room.

Bourne crashed through the doors and threw himself flat. Silence. Another scene from another hell. A section of the outside wall had been blown away. The owner and his cook were dead, blood streaming across the floor.

Bourne slowly rose to his feet, his legs in great pain. He looked through the smoke, his eyes finally settling on a large piece of paper fixed to the wall by a kitchen knife. He approached it and read the words, printed in black pen.

THE TREES OF TANNENBAUM WILL BURN AND SO WILL THE CHILDREN. SLEEP WELL, JASON BOURNE.

The mirrors of his life exploded into a thousand pieces of glass. There was nothing else to do except scream.

Chapter 12 The Apartment

The gray Citroen was parked a hundred meters away from the entrance of Dominique Lavier's apartment building on the fashionable Avenue Montaigne. Krupkin, Conklin, and Bourne sat in the back.

Sergei could be seen walking out of the glass doors. He crossed the wide street toward the Citroen, reached the car, and climbed in behind the wheel. "Everything is as it should be," he said, looking around. "The lady has not returned and the apartment is number twenty-one, second floor, right front side. It has been swept thoroughly; there are no hidden microphones."

"That makes sense. The Jackal could hardly have been checking personnel all over Paris. It all gets so complicated."

"I have arranged entry to Madame* Lavier's flat with the concierge. I have identified you all as belonging to the Deuxième."

"Good," said Krupkin. And then to Bourne and Conklin: "Let's go."

In the entrance hall, Krupkin nodded at the formally dressed concierge behind the counter.

"The door is open," said the concierge, avoiding direct eye contact.

Lavier's flat showed that she worked in the world of fashion. The walls were covered with photographs of people in the business attending important shows and events.

Both Conklin and the Russian immediately began examining the tables, picking up handwritten notes. Then Krupkin's radio suddenly gave out two sharp sounds.

"It must be Sergei," he said. "You're in place, comrade?"

"Yes." The assistant's quiet voice came from the radio. "The Lavier woman has just entered the building."

"Good … Alex, put the notes down. Lavier is coming."

The sound of a key turning a lock echoed through the living room. The three men turned to the door as a shocked Dominique Lavier walked inside. Her astonishment, however, was brief. She calmly replaced the key in her purse and spoke in English.

"Well, Kruppie, I might have known you were mixed up in this."

"Ah, the charming Jacqueline, or may we drop the pretence, Domie?"

* Madame: the French word for Mrs.

"*Kruppie*?" cried Conklin. "Domie?"

"Comrade Krupkin is one of the more public KGB officers in Paris," said Lavier, putting her purse on the table.

"It has its advantages," said Krupkin. "I understand you've met our tall American friend here, so I think it is only right I should introduce you to his friend, Aleksei Konsolikov."

"I don't believe you. He's not Soviet."

"You're right. He may introduce himself if he wishes to."

"The name's Conklin, Alex Conklin, Miss Lavier, and I'm American. However, my parents were Russian and I speak the language as well as they did, so my friend Krupkin can't deceive me when we're in Soviet company."

"I'm hurt," said Krupkin. "But that isn't important here. You will work with us, Domie?"

"I'll work with you, Kruppie. I only ask that Jason Bourne makes clear his offer to me. With Carlos I'm a caged animal, but without him I have no money."

"Name your price," said Bourne.

"Write it down," said Conklin, glancing at Krupkin.

"Let me see," said Lavier, walking across to the desk. "I'm within a few years of sixty—from one direction or the other—and I will have maybe fifteen to twenty years." She wrote a figure on a piece of paper and walked across to Bourne. "I'd prefer not to argue. I believe it's fair."

Bourne took the paper and read the amount: $1,000,000.00.

"It's fair," he said, handing the note back to Lavier. "Add how and where you want it paid and I'll make the arrangements when we leave here. The money will be there in the morning."

Lavier looked into Bourne's eyes. "I believe you," she said, bending over the desk and writing her instructions. She gave the paper back to him. "The deal is made, sir, and may God give us the kill. If He does not, *we* are dead."

Bourne nodded. "I've several questions," he said. "Do you want to sit down?"

"Yes." Lavier crossed to the sofa and settled into it.

"What happened at the Meurice Hotel?" said Bourne. "How did it happen?"

"Your woman—I assume it was your woman—screamed as you crossed the street. The rest you saw for yourself. How could you have told me to take a room at the Meurice knowing she was there?"

"I didn't know. We were here in Paris thirteen years ago ... My memory of that time isn't good, but the name Meurice means something. Maybe we stayed there—maybe that's why she chose it. Anyway, what is our position now?"

"Carlos still trusts me. He blames everything on the woman— your wife, I'm told—and has no reason to hold me responsible."

Bourne nodded. "How can you reach him?"

"I cannot directly. But I can get a message to him. I call several old men at cheap cafés, and they call others. Somehow the messages get through. Very quickly."

Conklin moved closer to her. "I want you to send the most urgent message you have ever sent to the Jackal. You *must* talk to him directly. It's an emergency and you can talk about it with nobody except Carlos himself."

"About what?" said Krupkin. "What could be so urgent that the Jackal will agree to a meeting? Like our Mr. Bourne, he worries about traps."

Conklin shook his head and limped to a side window, deep in thought. He looked down at the street. "My God, it could *work*," he whispered to himself.

"What could work?" asked Bourne.

"Dimitri, hurry. Call the embassy and have them send the biggest, most impressive limousine you have."

The force and urgency of Conklin's command had its effect. The Russian walked rapidly to the telephone and dialed, then spoke into the phone in Russian.

"It's done," said the KGB officer. "And now I think you should give me a good reason for doing it."

"Moscow," replied Conklin, still looking out the window.

"What are you *saying*?" roared Krupkin.

"We've got to get Carlos out of Paris," said Conklin, turning. "Where better than Moscow? In this city he's got all the firepower, an untraceable network of gunmen and messengers and many places to hide. London, Amsterdam, Brussels, Rome—they'd all be better for us, but the best is Moscow. Oddly, it's the one place in the world that he can't resist—and also the one that's the least welcoming."

"Alex, you're losing your mind," Krupkin said. "What could Domie say that would make him go to Moscow?"

"That's easy. The KGB in Moscow is getting closer to the Jackal's man in Dzerzhinsky Square. They know he's one of, let's say, ten or fifteen officers in the highest ranks. When they find him, Carlos can't do anything with the KGB—worse, he'll lose an informer who knows much too much about him to the men who ask painful questions."

"But how would Domie know that?" said Krupkin.

"Come over here," Conklin said. "Just you, for the moment, and stay away from the window. Look around the side of one of the curtains." The Soviet did as he was told. "What do you see?" asked Conklin, gesturing to an old brown car below on the street.

Krupkin did not bother to reply. Instead, he took his radio from his pocket and pressed a button. "Sergei, there's a brown car about eighty meters down the street—"

"We know, sir," interrupted the assistant. "We're watching it. It's an old man who hardly moves except to look out of the window."

"Does he have a car telephone?"

"No, comrade, and if he leaves the car he'll be followed, so there can be no outside calls unless you direct otherwise."

"Thank you, Sergei."

"The Jackal's man," said Bourne, stepping forward.

"Now, do you understand?" asked Conklin, speaking to Krupkin.

"Of course," replied the KGB official. "After we leave, Carlos is told that a Soviet embassy vehicle was sent to pick us up, and for what other reason would we be here except to question Madame Lavier? Naturally, with me was a tall man who might be Jason Bourne, and another shorter man with a disabled leg—so confirming that it *was* Jason Bourne. Our connection is therefore made and observed, and again, naturally, during our questioning of Madame Lavier, tempers rose and references were made to the Jackal's informer in Dzerzhinsky Square."

"Which only *I'd* known about through dealing with Santos at the Soldier's Heart," said Bourne quietly. "So Dominique has a believable observer—an old man from Carlos's army of old men—to support the information she delivers. Alex, that brain of yours hasn't lost its power."

"I hear a professor I once knew. I thought he'd left us."

"He has."

"Not for long, I hope."

Chapter 13 Moscow

Buckingham Pritchard sat next to his uniformed uncle, Cyril Sylvester Pritchard, Deputy Director of Immigration, in the office of the Crown Governor*, Sir Henry Sykes, at Government

* the Crown Governor: the British Queen's representative

House on the island of Montserrat. Beside them, on the deputy director's right, was their attorney, the finest local lawyer Sykes could persuade to advise the Pritchards if a case was brought against them for helping terrorists: Jonathan Lemuel, now retired after many years of experience in the highest English courts. Sir Henry sat behind his desk and glanced in shock at Lemuel, who raised his eyes to the ceiling in disbelief.

The cause of Sir Henry's shock and Jonathan Lemuel's disbelief was the result of the following exchange between Sykes and the Deputy Director of Immigration:

"Mr. Pritchard, you've admitted that your nephew overheard a telephone conversation between John St. Jacques and his brother-in-law, the American, Mr. David Webb. Also, your nephew Buckingham Pritchard admits calling you with certain information contained in that conversation. You then told him that you had to contact Paris immediately. Is this true?

"It is all *completely* true, Sir Henry."

"Whom did you reach in Paris? What's the telephone number?"

"With respect, sir, I am sworn to secrecy."

"*What* did you say, Mr. Pritchard?"

"My nephew and I are part of an international organization involving the great leaders of the world, and we have been sworn to secrecy."

"*Enough*!" shouted Sykes, the veins in his head standing out. "You have both been complete fools! You've been tricked by an international terrorist who is wanted all over the world! Do you know the penalty for helping such a killer? It is death by hanging. Now what's that number in Paris?"

"Under the circumstances," said the deputy director, speaking calmly despite the fact that his hand shook as he reached for his notebook, "I'll write it down for you. One asks for a blackbird. In French, Sir Henry."

♦

As Krupkin entered Moscow's Hotel Metropole with Bourne and Conklin, the manager quietly said, "Comrade! There is an urgent message for you." He walked rapidly up to the KGB man and pushed a folded note into his hand. "I was told to deliver it to you personally."

"You have done so and I thank you." Krupkin watched the man walk away, then opened the paper. "I must call Dzerzhinsky immediately," he said, turning. "It's the extension number of my assistant. Come, let's hurry."

In the suite, the doors of the two bedrooms were opposite each other; the space between them was a large sitting room complete with a bar.

"Help yourselves," said Krupkin, heading for a telephone on the desk. "By the way, you'll find your weapons in your bedside table drawers. Each is a .38 Graz Burya automatic."

Krupkin dialed a number and spoke in Russian. He shook his head as he hung up the telephone. "We must go immediately."

"Go where?" Conklin said. "We've just got here."

"We've taken an apartment on the Sadovaya—that's Moscow's widest street, Mr. Bourne. We'll be using it as our headquarters."

The car was parked some way from the hotel, where it would be less obvious. A hotel employee got it for them, and Krupkin drove them across the city.

The luxury apartment on the busy Sadovaya was one of many in an old stone building that, like the Hotel Metropole, reflected old Russia. The walls were covered with red wallpaper and the furniture was elegant, but to the right of the large living-room fireplace was a more modern item: a large black television set with a video cassette player.

In the apartment was a strongly built man in an untidy uniform, his shirt open at the neck.

"For you I have no name," he said. "You can call me Captain, although my rank is higher." The KGB officer walked to the huge television set and switched it on.

"St. Basil's in Red Square," said Krupkin, looking at the screen. "It's a museum now, but occasionally they hold a small religious service."

The screen shook as the man carrying the video camera moved inside the building. Then it became steady. It showed an elderly man in a black raincoat. He was walking beside one of the side walls.

"Rodchenko," said the captain. "The *great* Rodchenko."

The man on the screen moved into a corner where two large candles threw shadows on the stone walls. Rodchenko approached another man, a priest—losing his hair, thin, his skin dark.

"It's him!" cried Bourne. "It's *Carlos!*"

Then a third man appeared on the screen, joining the other two, and Conklin shouted. "*My God!*" he roared. "Hold it there!" The KGB officer paused the tape. "The *other* one! Do you recognize him, David?"

"I know him, but I don't know him," replied Bourne quietly, as images going back years began filling his mind. There were explosions, white blinding lights with figures running in a jungle. A captain with a Snake Lady tattooed on his arm.

"It's *Ogilvie!*" said Conklin, his voice distant. "Bryce Ogilvie … My God, they *did* link up. Medusa found the Jackal!"

Chapter 14 A Gunfight

In his bedroom at the Hotel Metropole, Conklin quickly replaced the telephone. Taking his Graz Burya automatic out of the bedside table drawer and pushing it into his belt, he crossed to the living-room door. Bourne was standing in front of a window.

"Was that Krupkin?" asked Bourne.

"It was. Move away from there."

"Carlos?" Bourne immediately stepped back and turned to Conklin. "He knows we're in Moscow?" he asked. Then added, "He knows where we are?"

"The answers are yes to both questions. Last night he killed Rodchenko, and also Krupkin's two agents who were following him."

"God, he's gone mad. But why do you think—?"

"One of the agents suffered a lot of pain before he died. He was our driver from the airport. He was also the son of a friend of Krupkin's—not trained for what he had to suffer. Krupkin thinks he probably talked."

"I'm sorry about the loss of life—I mean that. I wish it could have happened another way," said Bourne.

"We can't do anything about that now. Krupkin's on his way with an assault team, but he hasn't told the hotel staff. The place has to look normal."

"Yes, we'll take him here." Bourne noticed the gun in Conklin's belt. He gestured at the weapon. "That's a little obvious, isn't it?"

"For whom?"

"Room service," replied Bourne. "I phoned for some breakfast and a large pot of coffee."

"No. I promised Krupkin that we wouldn't let anybody in here."

"That's ridiculous."

"Almost my words, but this is his country, not ours."

"Wait a minute!" said Bourne. "Suppose he's right?"

Bourne reached under his jacket, pulled out his own Graz

Burya, and started for the hallway door of the suite.

"What are you doing?" cried Conklin.

"Get over there," ordered Bourne, pointing to the far left corner of the room. "I'll leave the door unlocked, and when the steward gets here, tell him to come in—in Russian."

"What about you?"

"There's a recess down the hall. I'll wait there."

Bourne opened the door, glanced up and down the passage, and rushed out. He raced to the recess, occupied by a Pepsi machine, and crouched by the right interior wall. He waited, his knees and legs aching—pains he never felt a few years ago—and then he heard the sounds of rolling wheels. They grew louder and louder as a cart covered with a tablecloth passed and moved to the door of the suite. The floor steward was a young man in his twenties, blond and short. Cautiously, he knocked on the door. Not Carlos, thought Bourne, getting painfully to his feet. He could hear Conklin's voice telling the steward to enter, and as the young man opened the door, pushing the cart inside, Bourne calmly replaced his weapon. He bent over, rubbing his right leg.

It happened suddenly. A figure in black came out of an unseen recess farther down the passage, racing past the machine. Bourne spun back into the wall. It was the *Jackal*!

Madness! At full force, Carlos hit the steward with his right shoulder, pushing the young man across the hallway and crashing the cart over on its side, food and coffee spilling across the carpeted floor. Suddenly, the steward moved to his left as, astonishingly, he pulled a weapon from his belt. The Jackal either sensed or caught the movement in the corner of his eye. He spun around, his machine pistol on rapid fire, pinning the blond Russian into the wall, bullets tearing through the steward's head and body. In that long, horrible moment, the barrel of Bourne's Graz Burya caught in the waistline of his pants. He tore the fabric as the eyes of Carlos swept up, centering on his own, anger and victory in the assassin's stare.

Bourne pulled the gun loose, spinning, crouching back into the small recess as the Jackal's bullets blew apart the front of the soft drink machine. On his stomach, Bourne moved across the opening, the Graz Burya raised, and firing as fast as he could. At the same time there were other gunshots, not those of a machine pistol. Conklin was firing from inside the suite! They had Carlos in their cross fire! It was possible—it could all end in a hotel passage in Moscow! Let it happen, *let it happen*!

The Jackal roared, angry at having been hit. Bourne threw himself back into the recess. Again he crouched. Like an angry, caged animal, the wounded Carlos kept firing bursts from his weapon. Two frightened screams came from the far end of the hallway, one male, one female. A couple had been wounded or killed in the storm of bullets.

"Get down!" Conklin screamed from across the passage. "Take cover!"

Bourne did as he was told, pushing himself into the corner of the recess, protecting his head as much as possible. The first explosion shook the walls—somewhere—and then a second one, much nearer, in the hallway itself. Grenades!

Smoke mixed with the broken glass. Gunshots. Nine, one after another—a Graz Burya automatic … *Alex!* Bourne got up from the corner of the recess and moved through the opening. Conklin stood outside the door of their suite. He searched the pockets of his pants.

"He ran around the corner into the other passage. My gun's empty and I don't have any more bullets!"

"I do and I'm a lot faster than you," said Bourne, reloading his gun. "Get back in there and call downstairs. Tell them to clear the area."

"Krupkin said—"

"I don't care what he said! Tell them to shut down the elevators, close all stair exits, and stay away from this floor!"

Bourne raced down the hallway, slowing as he approached the couple who lay on the carpet. Each moved in pain. Their clothes were spotted with blood, but they moved! He turned and shouted to Conklin.

"Get help up through here!" he ordered, pointing at an exit door down the passage. "They're alive!"

He moved on, but he knew already that it was too late to catch up with Carlos.

♦

A day later, Bourne, Conklin, and Krupkin sat in the living room of the hotel suite, waiting for news. The door opened and the KGB officer who called himself a captain entered. He looked at the three men and spat out one word: "Novgorod!"

"What?" the men cried together.

"You," the officer addressed Bourne, switching to English. "You understood?"

"I know the name," Bourne said.

"He broke into a weapons store at Kubinka. He killed the staff there—though some escaped. He stole guns, plastic explosives, heat-seeking missiles... The store is on the road to Novgorod."

"He's going back to the place of his 'birth,'" said Krupkin. "To the training camp where Ilich Ramirez Sanchez became Carlos the Jackal. He's going there because he was thrown out, marked for death as a madman."

"What will he do in Novgorod?" asked Bourne quietly.

"Who knows? He intends to leave his mark, no doubt, in answer to the people he believes betrayed him more than thirty years ago. He probably has papers to get him inside—I can't believe he hasn't. But we'll stop him."

"Don't even try," said Bourne. "He may or may not use the papers. Like me, he doesn't need them to get inside, but if he senses something is wrong, and he will, he'll kill a number of good men and still get in."

"What are you saying?" asked Krupkin cautiously.

"Get me inside ahead of him with a detailed map of the whole complex and a document that allows me to go wherever I want to."

"You've lost your senses!" cried Krupkin. "An American, an assassin, inside *Novgorod*?"

"I haven't the slightest interest in your training facility. My only concern is Carlos. I want him dead—and so do you."

"All right," said Conklin, from his chair, his eyes on the ceiling. He looked straight at Krupkin. "Let's deal. You get him into Novgorod and you keep Ogilvie."

"We've already got him, Aleksei."

"You haven't. Washington knows he's here."

"So?"

"So I can say you lost him and they'll believe me. Think of it: no World Court embarrassments, none of the problems caused by holding an American accused of international crimes. You take over the Medusa operation with no complications, and who better to be in charge than you, a cultured man with experience of living in the West? Forget the house in Geneva, Kruppie, how about a villa on the Black Sea?"

"It is a most intelligent and attractive offer," said Krupkin thoughtfully.

"No, no, no!" shouted the KGB officer. "This is crazy!"

"Oh, for God's sake, shut up!" roared Krupkin. "We're talking about things you cannot possibly understand."

"What?" Like a young child criticized by an adult, the officer was both surprised and frightened by Krupkin's words.

"Very well," said Krupkin, his own eyes now on the ceiling.

"The order will be issued secretly, its origins untraceable."

"How fast can I get there?" asked Bourne. "There's a lot I have to organize."

"We have an airport in Vnokova under our control, no more than an hour away. First, I must make arrangements. Hand me a telephone … You, my stupid comrade!" The officer moved quickly, bringing a phone to Krupkin's table.

"One more thing," Bourne said. "Have Tass* put out an immediate news release with heavy coverage in the newspapers, radio, and television that the assassin known as Jason Bourne died of his wounds here in Moscow. Don't give too much detail, but they will need to know something of what happened here this morning."

"That's not difficult. Tass is an obedient servant of the state."

Chapter 15 Novgorod

Novgorod. It was a work of great inventiveness cut out of the immense forests along the Volkhov River. From the moment Bourne appeared from the deep underground tunnel below the water, with its guards, gates, and many cameras, he was close to being in a state of shock.

The American compound, presumably like those of the other countries, was broken up into sections, built on areas up to a kilometer square, each distinctly separate from the others. One area, on the banks of the river, might be the heart of a Maine village by the ocean; another, further inland, a small Southern town; another, a busy city street. Each was completely "real," with the appropriate vehicles, police, stores and drugstores, gas stations, and office buildings. The people

* Tass: the official news service of the Soviet Union

who worked there dressed as local people would.

Obviously, as important as the physical appearances was language—not just the use of excellent English, but the mastery of regional differences. As Bourne wandered from one section to another, he heard all around him the distinctive sounds of New England, of Texas, of the Midwest and the large Eastern cities. It was all unbelievable.

Bourne followed the signs—everything was in English—to the "city" of Rockledge, Florida. He was going to meet a man called Benjamin at a lunch counter in the local Woolworth store. He was looking for a man in his mid-twenties, with a Budweiser baseball cap on the high chair beside him, saving the place. It was time: three thirty-five in the afternoon.

He saw him. The sandy-haired Russian was seated at the far right end of the counter. There were half a dozen men and women along the row talking to one another over soft drinks and snacks. Bourne approached the empty seat, glanced down at the cap, and spoke politely. "Is this taken?" he asked.

"I'm waiting for somebody," replied the young KGB trainer.

"I'm just having a quick Coke. I'll be out of here in a few minutes."

"Sit down," said Benjamin, removing the hat and putting it on his head. A waiter came by and Bourne ordered. His drink arrived, and the KGB trainer continued quietly. "So you're Archie."

"And you're Benjamin. Nice to know you."

"We'll both find out if that's a fact, won't we?"

"Do we have a problem?"

"I don't approve of you being here. I've lived in the United States and I sound American, but I don't like Americans."

"Listen to me, Ben," interrupted Bourne, his eyes forcing the trainer to look at him. "I haven't the slightest interest in the purpose of Novgorod—although the whole complex is a lot more impressive than Disneyland." Benjamin tried hard not to laugh and failed. "Come on," said Bourne. "Let's take a walk."

Eight hours later, at exactly 12:02 A.M., the telephone in the Command Suite screamed. Benjamin leaped off the couch, and grabbed the phone. "Yes? … Where? When? And he's inside? … Yes!" He put the phone down and turned to Bourne. "It's unbelievable! At the Spanish tunnel—across the river two guards are dead, and on this side the officer of the guard was found fifty meters away from his post, a bullet in his throat. They ran the video tapes and all they saw was an unidentified man walking through carrying a bag! In a guard's *uniform*!"

"What else?" asked Bourne coldly.

"On the other side was a dead farm worker holding torn papers in his hand. He was lying between the two murdered guards, one of them only wearing his shorts and shoes … How did he *do* it?"

"The farm worker was working for him. Carlos must have paid him a lot and sent him in with rotten false papers, then run in himself. The officer appeared at the right time and caught the farm worker, and in the confusion Carlos got through the tunnel."

"But the papers he used—everything had to be checked against the computer. Those were Krupkin's instructions."

"I think you have to accept that Carlos has somebody inside here, somebody with authority."

"That's possible," agreed the young trainer rapidly.

"So let's go, and when we get outside we stop somewhere and you get me what I need."

"OK. That's been approved."

♦

The Jackal braked the huge fuel truck at the "West German" border. He adjusted the coarse shirt that covered a Spanish general's uniform, and as the guard came out of the gatehouse Carlos spoke in Russian, using the same words he had used at every other crossing.

"Don't ask me to speak the stupid language you talk here! I deliver gas, I don't spend time in classrooms! Here's my key."

"I barely speak it myself, comrade," said the guard, laughing as he accepted the small, flat object and pushed it into the computerized machine. The heavy iron barrier moved up into the vertical position; the guard returned the key and the Jackal sped through into a small "West Berlin."

In the narrow copy of a main street he slowed down and pulled the gas release. The fuel flowed out into the street. He then reached into the open bag on the seat beside him, took out the small, pre-timed plastic explosives, and as he had done throughout the southern compounds to the border of "France," threw them through the lowered windows on both sides of the truck toward the wooden buildings he thought would burn best. He sped into the "Munich" section, then to the port of "Bremerhaven" on the river, and finally into "Bonn," flooding the street, throwing out the explosives. He had barely fifteen minutes before the first explosions took place in all of "West Germany," followed by explosions in the other compounds, each spaced eight minutes apart, timed to create maximum effect.

And while the fire engines raced here and there, and the frightened people tried to escape, Ilich Ramirez Sanchez would burn "Paris." Then would come "England" and finally, the largest compound in Novgorod, the "United States of America," country of the second-rate assassin, Jason Bourne.

Carlos checked his bag. What remained were the most dangerous instruments of death found in the weapons store of Kubinka—four rows of short heat-seeking missiles, twenty in all. When they were sent into the sky, each would seek the sources of fire and do its work.

♦

Bourne stopped the jeep at the entrance to the French compound and handed the guard his computerized card. "Quickly, please," he said in French.

The guard walked rapidly to the security machine as an enormous fuel truck, heading the other way, passed through into "England."

The guard returned and the iron barrier was raised. Bourne accelerated, and saw in a matter of moments a three-floor copy of the Eiffel Tower.

"Slow down," said Benjamin, touching his arm.

"What is it?"

"Stop!" cried the young trainer. "Shut off the engine."

Bourne drove to the side of the road and switched off. "What's the matter with you?"

Benjamin was looking around him, his eyes on the clear night sky. "No clouds," he said. "No storms."

"So what? I want to get up to the Spanish compound."

"There it goes again." Now Bourne heard it … far away, the sound of distant thunder, but the night was clear. It happened again—and again and again, one deep sound after another.

"*There!*" shouted the young Soviet, standing up in the jeep and pointing to the north. "What *is* it?"

"That's fire, young man," answered Bourne softly, as he also stood up and stared at the yellow light in the distant sky. "And my guess is it's the Spanish compound. He was initially trained there and that's what he came back to do—to blow the place *up*! It's his revenge! … Get down, we've got to get up there!"

"No, you're wrong," Benjamin interrupted, quickly lowering himself into the seat as Bourne started the engine and pulled the jeep into gear. "Spain's no more than eight kilometers from here. Those fires are a lot farther away."

"Just show me the fastest route," said Bourne, pressing the accelerator to the floor.

As they came in sight of the "Spanish" border, the explosions were louder and the night sky turned a brighter shade of yellow. The guards at the gate were talking quickly into their telephones and hand-held radios; the sounds of police cars and fire engines were joining the shouting and the screaming.

"What's *happening?*" shouted Benjamin, leaping from the jeep and speaking Russian. "I'm senior staff!" he added, slipping the card into the release equipment, sending the barrier up. "*Tell* me!"

"Madness, comrade!" shouted an officer from the gatehouse window. "Unbelievable! ... First, West Germany—all over there are explosions and fires in the streets and buildings going up in flames. Then it happens in Italy—Rome burns down—and in the Greek section, and still the explosions continue."

Another wall phone rang inside the gatehouse; the officer of the guard picked it up, then screamed at the top of his lungs, "Madness, it's complete *madness!* Are you certain?"

"What is it?" roared Benjamin, rushing to the window.

"Egypt!" he screamed, his ear pressed to the telephone. "Israel! ... Fires everywhere, bombs everywhere!"

"Get back here!" shouted Bourne.

Benjamin ran to the jeep and jumped in as Bourne accelerated through the gate.

"It was the fuel truck, that damned fuel truck that passed us at the French border. That was *him!*"

"Yes—but where are we going?" Benjamin shouted.

"It'll end in the American compound. It has to."

The copy of the White House fell in flames and "Pennsylvania Avenue" was on fire. Bourne stopped the jeep in the street beside the river, and again there were frightened crowds. The police were shouting through loudspeakers, first in English, then in Russian, explaining that the river was wired and that the electricity would kill anybody trying to swim across. The searchlights showed the floating bodies of those who had tried this in the northern compounds.

"The tunnel, the *tunnel! Open the tunnel!*"

Bourne leaped out of the jeep, pocketing three flares, and fought his way through the crowds. Benjamin ran after him. *There!* In the fenced-off parking lot was the fuel truck! He broke through the guards, holding up his computerized release card, and ran up to a captain with an AK-47 on his waist.

"My identification is with the name 'Archie' and you can check it immediately."

"Of course we know of you," the officer cried, "but what can I *do*? This is an uncontrollable situation!"

"Has anybody passed through the tunnel in the last half hour?"

"No one, absolutely *no* one! Our orders are to keep it closed!"

"Good. Get on the loudspeakers and tell the crowds to break up. Tell them the crisis has passed and the danger with it."

"How *can* I? The fires are everywhere, the explosions *everywhere!*"

"Do as he *says!*" roared Benjamin's voice behind Bourne.

"Who *gives* me such orders?" shouted the officer.

"Check my authority, friend, but do it quickly," answered Benjamin, holding out his card. "*Move*, you fool!"

"Attention!" The voice came from the many loudspeakers around the tunnel, as the explosions began to die down. "The crisis has passed. Stay by the banks of the river and we will look after you. These are orders from our superiors, comrades."

"But we're being *attacked!*" shouted a man at the front of the panicked crowd.

"Open the tunnel and let us out or you'll have to shoot us down! Open the *tunnel!*" the people cried.

The protesting voices grew louder.

"Can you operate the tunnel's machinery?" Bourne shouted.

"Yes! Everybody on the senior staff can—it's part of the job."

"The iron gates you told me about?"

"Of course."

"Where are the controls?"

"The guardhouse."

"Get in there!" shouted Bourne to Benjamin, taking one of the flares out of his field-jacket pocket and handing it to him. "When you see one of my flares go over the crowd, lower those gates on *this side—only* this side, understood?"

"What for?"

"*My rules*, Ben! *Do* it! Then light this flare and throw it out the window so I'll know it's done."

"Then what?"

"Something you may not want to do, but you have to ... Take the gun from the captain's body and force the crowd, *shoot* it back into the street. Rapid fire into the ground in front of them—or above them. Do whatever you have to do."

The trainer named Benjamin looked angrily at Bourne, then turned and began fighting his way to the guardhouse. Bourne studied the fenced parking area, counting the other vehicles in addition to the fuel truck. There were nine parked by the fence—six cars and three vans, all American-made or good copies.

Bourne crouched and crawled forward. He reached the waist-high fence, the noise behind him continuous, deafening. Then, from an opening he could not see, two police cars raced inside. Uniformed men leaped out from every door and ran to the open gate that led to the guardhouse and tunnel.

There was a break in space, in *time.* In *men!* Three men had come out of the second car but now there were four—but he was not the same—the uniform was not the same! The officer's cap had a gold ribbon and the shape was wrong for the

US Army. What *was* it? … And suddenly, Bourne understood. His memory went back years to Madrid. It was a *Spanish* uniform. That was it! Carlos had entered through the Spanish compound, and as his Russian was excellent, he was using the high-ranking uniform to make his escape from Novgorod.

Bourne got to his feet, his automatic in his hand, and ran across the lot, his left hand reaching into his field jacket pocket for a flare. He pulled the release and threw it above the cars. Benjamin would not see it from the guardhouse and mistake it for the signal to close the gates of the tunnel.

"*Look out!*" roared one of the escaping men, turning around and panicked at the sight of the blinding flare.

"*Run!*" shouted another, racing toward the open section of the fence. Bourne counted the seven figures as one by one they ran away from the last car and passed through the opening, joining the excited crowds at the mouth of the tunnel. The eighth man did not appear; the Spanish officer's uniform was not in sight. The Jackal was trapped!

Now! Bourne took out a flare, pulled the release, and threw it with all his strength at the guardhouse. *Do it, Ben!* he screamed in silence as he took out the last grenade. *Do it now!*

A thunderous roar came from the tunnel, frightened protests from the crowd, then two rapid bursts of automatic gunfire were followed by commands over the speakers, shouted in Russian.

Bourne dropped to the ground, looking at the undersides of the vehicles. A pair of legs—in *boots*! Behind the third car on the left. He gripped the grenade in his right hand, pulled the pin, and threw it under the car toward the legs—only at the last moment realizing that he had made a terrible *error!* The legs behind the car did not move—the boots remained in place, because they were only *boots!* Bourne threw himself away from the car, onto the ground, and curled his body into the smallest mass he could manage.

The explosion was deafening, pieces of glass and metal stinging Bourne's back and legs. He got to his feet in the smoke and fire. As he did so, the ground was torn up around him. He ran toward the protection of the nearest vehicle, a square-shaped van. He was hit twice, in the shoulder and thigh!

"You're nothing compared to me, Jason Bourne!" screamed Carlos the Jackal, his automatic weapon on rapid fire. "You never *were!* You're a pretender, a *fraud!*"

"Then come and get me!" Bourne moved to the driver's door, pulled it open, then ran to the back of the vehicle where he crouched, his face to the edge, his Colt .45 next to his cheek. The Jackal stopped his continuous fire. Bourne understood. Carlos faced the open door, unsure, indecisive … only seconds to go. Metal against metal, a gun barrel was pushed against the door, shutting it. *Now!*

Bourne spun around the edge of the van, his weapon firing into the Spanish uniform, blowing the gun out of the Jackal's hands. *One, two, three*; the bullets flew through the air—and then they stopped! They *stopped*, as the gun stuck, refusing to fire. Carlos dropped to the ground for his weapon, his left arm limp and bleeding but his right hand still strong.

Bourne pulled out his knife and leaped forward, slicing the blade down toward the Jackal's arm. He was too late! Carlos held the weapon! Bourne's hand held the hot barrel—hold on, hold *on! You can't let it go! Twist it! Use the knife!*

With a last desperate effort, Bourne pushed up and crashed Carlos back into the side of the van, striking his wounded shoulder again and again. The Jackal screamed, dropping the weapon, then kicked it under the van.

Where the blow came from, Bourne at first did not know; he only knew that the left side of his head seemed suddenly to split in two. Then he realized that he had done it to himself!

He had slipped on the blood-covered ground, and had crashed into the side of the van. It did not matter—*nothing* mattered!

Carlos the Jackal was racing away! With the confusion everywhere, there were a hundred ways he could get out of Novgorod. It had all been for *nothing*!

Still, there was his last grenade. Why not? Bourne removed it, pulled the pin, and threw it over the van into the center of the parking area. The explosion followed and Bourne got to his feet. Maybe the grenade would tell Benjamin something, warn him to keep his eyes on the area.

Barely able to walk, Bourne started for the break in the fence that led to the guardhouse and the tunnel. *Oh, God, Marie, I failed! I'm so sorry. Nothing! It was all for nothing!* And then, as if all Novgorod were having a final laugh at his expense, he saw that somebody had opened the iron gates to the tunnel, giving the Jackal his invitation to freedom.

"*Archie …?*" The young Soviet ran out of the guardhouse toward Bourne. "God, I thought you were *dead!*"

"So you opened the gates to let my killer walk away," shouted Bourne weakly. "Why didn't you send a limousine for him?"

"I suggest you look again, Professor," replied a breathless Benjamin, studying Bourne's bruised face and bloodstained clothing. "Old age has damaged your eyesight."

"What?"

"You want gates, you'll have gates." The trainer shouted an order toward the guardhouse in Russian. Seconds later the huge iron gates descended, covering the mouth of the tunnel. But something was strange. The gates appeared to be … swollen somehow, shiny and showing reflections. "Glass," said Benjamin.

"Glass?" asked a puzzled Bourne.

"At each end of the tunnel, eight-centimeter walls of glass, locked up."

"What are you talking about?" It was not necessary for the

young Russian to explain. Suddenly, a series of huge waves crashed against the glass as the tunnel filled with the waters of the Volkhov River. Then, within the silence of the growing, moving liquid, there was an object—a thing, a body! Bourne stared in shock, unable to release the cry that was in him. He gathered what strength he had left and ran unsteadily to the wall of glass. Breathlessly, he placed his hands against it and looked at the scene barely centimeters in front of him. The dead body of Carlos the Jackal kept crashing back and forward into the steel bars of the gate, his features twisted in hate.

Jason Bourne watched in satisfaction, his mouth tight—the face of a killer, a killer among killers, who had won. Briefly, however, the softer eyes of David Webb appeared, forming the face of a man for whom the weight of a world he hated had been removed.

Activities

Chapter 1

Before you read

1 Read the Introduction. Discuss the order in which these events in David Webb's life happened.

. **a** He married Marie.
b He went to Hong Kong.
c He was shot in the head and lost his memory.
d A plane killed his first wife and their children.
e He met and killed the original Jason Bourne.
f His employers in the United States tried to kill him.
g He worked in Cambodia for the CIA.
h He joined a secret special operations group known as Medusa.

2 Now match these dates to events in Robert Ludlum's life.

1927 1945 the 1950s 1971 the mid-1970s 2001

a His first novel, *The Scarlatti Inheritance*, appeared.
b He was born in New York City.
c He died.
d He began to serve as a soldier in the South Pacific.
e He became a full-time writer.
f He worked as a stage and television actor.

3 Look at the Word List at the back of the book. Check the meanings of words that are new to you. Then:

a find two types of vehicles.
b find two things that can explode.
c find three places where people can live or stay.

While you read

4 Match the people with their jobs (1–6).

a Alex Conklin ....
b Morris Panov ....
c David Webb ....
d Peter Holland ....
e Casset ....
f Steven DeSole ....

1 a deputy director of Central Intelligence
2 the Director of Central Intelligence
3 the keeper of CIA files
4 a retired CIA officer
5 a psychiatrist
6 a university professor

After you read

5 Decide whether these sentences are true ✓ or false ✗.

a Jason Bourne sent a message to Conklin and Panov. ....
b Conklin has an injured leg. ....
c Marie's brother owns half of a hotel. ....
d Conklin has never met Peter Holland before. ....
e Conklin thinks a secret file has been opened. ....
f DeSole's job has changed in recent years. ....
g Conklin has worked with Edward McAllister. ....
h Carlos the Jackal tried to kill Conklin in the amusement park. ....

Chapters 2–3

Before you read

6 Find the places below on a map. Which of them are in:

a the People's Republic of China?
b the Caribbean?
c the United States?
d Vietnam?
e France?

Boston Hong Kong Marseilles Montserrat Paris
Saigon Virginia Washington, D.C.

While you read

7 Decide whether these people are part of Medusa (M), or work for the Jackal (J).

a Albert Armbruster ....
b Phillip Atkinson ....
c Jonathan Burton ....
d "Jean Pierre Fontaine" ....
e Randolph Gates ....
f Norman Swayne ....
g James Teagarten ....

After you read

8 Medusa is a network involving people in high positions in the United States. In other kinds of networks, members may have gone to the same school or university, or belong to the same club or society. Discuss powerful networks in your country.

9 Use a library or the Internet to find more about the U.S. Senate, the Pentagon, NATO, and Harvard University.

Chapters 4–5

Before you read

10 Which one of these do you think will happen when Bourne visits General Swayne's farm?

- **a** He will be captured by the general's guards.
- **b** The general will shoot Bourne.
- **c** Somebody will shoot the general.
- **d** The general will tell Bourne all about Medusa.

While you read

11 Number these things in the order that Bourne uses them on General Swayne's farm.

a	a cart	....	**e**	a telephone	....
b	a dart gun	....	**f**	an automatic	....
c	a fallen branch	....	**g**	binoculars	....
d	a surgical glove	....	**h**	wire cutters	....

After you read

12 *"Would you have killed me?" asked Marie.*
"If I had not seen the needles? I simply don't know."
Explain what Marie and Fontaine are talking about. Should Marie be discussing this with him, or should she call the police and have him arrested? Discuss your ideas.

Chapters 6–7

Before you read

13 The Jackal is coming to the island of Tranquility. What preparations do you think Bourne will make for the safety of Marie and the children, and to find and kill him? Think about this, write down some ideas, then read the chapter.

While you read

14 One word in each sentence is wrong. Cross it out and write the correct word.

- **a** Marie and the children leave the island by helicopter. ....
- **b** Bourne and Prefontaine watch the hotel grounds and wait for the Jackal. ....
- **c** Three guards are killed on the beach, each with a bullet in his heart. ....
- **d** Fontaine's brother works for the Jackal. ....
- **e** Fontaine is killed by a bomb outside the church. ....
- **f** Bourne saved Bernardine's life. ....
- **g** Teagarten is killed in a restaurant. ....
- **h** The name Jason Bourne is written in blood. ....

After you read

15 Decide who you think is responsible for each of these events. Discuss your ideas with another student.

- **a** Fontaine's death
- **b** Swayne's death
- **c** Panov's kidnapping
- **d** Bernardine's meeting with Bourne
- **e** DeSole's death
- **f** Teagarten's death

Chapters 8–9

Before you read

16 These places are mentioned in Chapters 8 and 9. Find them on a map of Paris.

Montparnasse   Argenteuil   the Pont-Royal Hotel
the meeting of the Rue du Bac and the Rue de Montalambert
Orly Airport   the river Seine   the Boulevard Lefébvre.

While you read

17 Match two people with each sentence.

Bernardine   Bourne   DeFazio   Gates   Ogilvie   Panov
Prefontaine   Santos

- **a** They have marks on their arms. ....
....

b They do a deal to kill Bourne. ....

....

c They give information about Marseilles. ....

....

d They are given a telephone number. ....

....

After you read

18 Answer these questions:

a What is the Spanish connection between the Jackal and the manager of The Soldier's Heart?

b Which words does Bernardine use that show his English is upper class?

c How do we know Panov isn't interested in U.S. history?

d Santos has two hobbies. What are they?

19 Louis DeFazio lives in Brooklyn. Bryce Ogilvie works for a law firm in Manhattan. Find out where these two places are, how they are different and what this might say about the social backgrounds of the two men.

Chapters 10–11

Before you read

20 Bourne is walking into a trap. What do you think will happen?

a Carlos will kill him.

b He will kill Carlos.

c He will try to kill Carlos but Carlos will escape.

d Bernardine will reach him before he gets near Carlos.

21 Look at the facts below. How do you think they will affect the story in these two chapters? Discuss your ideas.

a Santos will not leave Paris without his collection of books.

b Bernardine has friends and contacts in the Paris police.

c Carlos was brought up in the Roman Catholic Church.

d The last time Bourne and Marie were in Paris, thirteen years before, they stayed in the Meurice Hotel.

e Conklin has an old KGB friend in Paris.

f Carlos was trained in the Soviet Union.

While you read

22 Which person is speaking?

Bernardine Bourne Conklin Krupkin Dominique Lavier Johnny St. Jacques Marie Panov

a "For God's sake, what *happened*?" ....

b "She knew the rules. She betrayed him." ....

c "I'll call in the Deuxième." ....

d "My God, is he *here*?" ....

e "Call me in five or six hours." ....

f "No American is going to order me and your kids around." ....

g "You're the only support he's got." ....

h "So I have the honor to meet the famous Jason Bourne." ....

After you read

23 Join the two halves of the sentences. In which order did the events happen?

a If Bourne hadn't met Dominique Lavier …

b If Bernardine hadn't been killed …

c If Bourne hadn't gone to the Boulevard Lefébvre ...

d If he hadn't sent Lavier to the Meurice Hotel ...

e If Bernardine hadn't spoken to Conklin ...

1) he wouldn't have met Dominique Lavier.

2) Bernardine wouldn't have been killed.

3) he wouldn't have gone to the Boulevard Lefébvre.

4) Bourne and Marie wouldn't have left Paris.

5) he wouldn't have sent her to the Meurice Hotel.

Chapters 12–13

Before you read

24 Which of these will we learn next? Circle your best guesses.

a Conklin's parents were *Russian/French.*

b Lavier knows *Conklin/Krupkin* well.

c Carlos will go to *Moscow/New* York.

d Carlos has an employee with a high rank in the *KGB/Deuxième.*

e Bryce Ogilvie will meet the *Jackal/Panov.*

While you read

25 Who are these sentences about?

a "I might have known you were mixed up in this." ....

b "I don't believe you. He's not Soviet." ....

c "I will have maybe fifteen to twenty years." ....

d "In this city he's got all the firepower." ....

e "I hear a professor I once knew ... I thought he'd left us." ....

f "You have both been complete fools!" ....

g "I know him but I don't know him." ....

After you read

26 *"Bryce Ogilvie ... My God, they did link up. Medusa found the Jackal!"*
Imagine that, after this, Conklin explains what he means to Krupkin. Act out their conversation with another student. Make sure that Krupkin understands everything about Medusa.

Chapters 14–15

Before you read

27 In Chapter 14, Carlos comes to the hotel where Bourne and Conklin are staying. Imagine that you are Carlos. What would your plan be?

While you read

28 Use one number to complete each sentence.

two three nine twenty thirty thirty-five

a On the previous night, Carlos shot .... men.

b He injures .... guests in the hotel.

c Conklin fires .... shots at Carlos with the automatic.

d Carlos was last in Novgorod more than .... years before.

e Bourne meets Benjamin at three ....

f Carlos has .... heat-seeking missiles.

After you read

29 Decide whether these sentences are true or false.

- **a** Carlos kills Krupkin's nephew.
- **b** The floor steward fires at Carlos.
- **c** Carlos is wounded in the hotel.
- **d** Years ago, the staff at Novgorod thought Carlos was insane.
- **e** Carlos enters Novgorod with false papers.
- **f** Some people swim across the river to escape the fires.
- **g** Carlos got himself a uniform in the Spanish compound.
- **h** Bourne watches Carlos die in the tunnel.

30 Which of these weapons are used by Bourne, by Carlos, or by both of them?

- **a** Graz Burya automatic
- **b** grenade
- **c** plastic explosive
- **d** heat-seeking missile
- **e** Colt .45
- **f** knife

Writing

31 Use a library or the Internet to find out more about the life and work of Robert Ludlum and the movies that have been made of his books. Write a report.

32 Watch the movie of *The Bourne Ultimatum* on DVD. The settings and events are very different from the ones in the book. Why, do you think? Which story do you prefer? Write about this.

33 After the shooting at the amusement park, Conklin tells Panov to find a pay phone and tell Bourne to take Marie and the children and leave home. Write the conversation between Panov and Bourne.

34 Use the library or the Internet to find out more about France during World War II. How might somebody have become a hero of France at that time? Write a report.

35 Bourne sends Marie and the children to the Tranquility Hotel on a small island in the Caribbean. Imagine that an international assassin is trying to kill you. Where would you choose to hide? Would you go far away or hide in a local town or city that you know well? Write a plan.

36 *"I'll close for six months, change the name, then start advertising* *in the magazines before reopening," said John St. Jacques to his brother-in-law.*

Imagine it is now six months later. What new name do you think St. Jacques might have chosen for the hotel? How should he advertise it? Write a full-page advertisement for the reopening of the hotel.

37 After Panov escapes, Conklin asks him to write down everything he may have told while he was drugged. Conklin wants to know what might be a danger to Bourne. Write Panov's report.

38 Marie and Bourne are trying to find each other in Paris. Today this would not be difficult. Write about changes in technology and communication since this book was written, in the late 1980s, and today.

39 Use a library or the Internet to find out about the Soviet Union (1922–91), and its security service, the KGB. Write a report.

40 At the end of the story, Bourne is inside the Soviet Union. He knows too much about Novgorod, and the Soviet government would probably prefer him dead. Krupkin can help him, and might decide to leave, too. Write the story of what happens.

WORD LIST

assassin (n) somebody who murders an important person or important people, often for political reasons or for money

barrel (n) the part of a gun that the bullets are fired through

binoculars (n pl) a pair of glasses used for looking at distant objects

cobra (n) a poisonous African or Asian snake that can spread the skin of its neck to make itself bigger

compound (n) an area that contains a group of buildings and is surrounded by a fence or wall

comrade (n) somebody who is a member of the same political party, used especially by people in Communist groups

concierge (n) somebody who looks after a building in France, usually by watching the entrance to see who comes in and goes out; somebody whose job in a hotel is helping guests, for example by giving them advice about local restaurants

cover (n) a disguise; shelter or protection from attack. **Coverage** on television or radio, or in newspapers, is the way in which news is reported.

crouch (v) to lower your body close to the ground by bending your knees

dart (n) a small pointed object that is shot as a weapon

flare (n) a piece of equipment that produces a bright flame, used as a signal

grenade (n) a small bomb that can be thrown by hand

hypodermic needle (n) an instrument with a very thin, hollow needle used for putting drugs directly into your body through your skin

immigration (n) the process of entering another country in order to live there

jackal (n) a wild animal like a dog that lives in Asia and Africa and eats the remaining parts of dead animals

jeep (n) a type of car made for traveling over rough ground

limousine (n) a big, expensive, comfortable car

limp (n/v) the way somebody walks, slowly and with difficulty, because one leg is hurt or injured